The Jerry McNeal Series

Star Treatment

(A Paranormal Snapshot)

By Sherry A. Burton

Dorry Press

***Clean and Cozy Jerry McNeal Series Collection
(Compilations of the standalone Jerry McNeal
series)***

*The Jerry McNeal Clean and Cozy Edition Volume
one (books 1-3)*
*The Jerry McNeal Clean and Cozy Edition Volume
two (books 4-6)*
*The Jerry McNeal Clean and Cozy Edition Volume
three (books 7-9)*
*The Jerry McNeal Clean and Cozy Edition Volume
four (books 10-12)*

Romance Books (*not clean** - sex and language)*
Tears of Betrayal
Love in the Bluegrass
Somewhere In My Dreams
The King of My Heart

***Romance Books** (clean)*
Seems Like Yesterday

"Whispers of the Past" (a short story)

Psychological Thriller
Surviving the Storm (Sex, Language, and Violence)

The Jerry McNeal Series
Star Treatment

By Sherry A. Burton

The Jerry McNeal Series: Star Treatment
Copyright 2023

By Sherry A. Burton
Published by Dorry Press
Edited and Formatted by BZHercules.com
Cover by Laura J. Prevost
@laurajprevostphotography
Proofread by Latisha Rich

For more information on the author and her works, please see www.SherryABurton.com

Acknowledgements

I will forever be grateful to my mom, who insisted the dog stay in the series.

To my hubby, thanks for helping me stay in the writing chair.

To my editor, Beth, for allowing me to keep my voice.

To Laura, for EVERYTHING you do to keep me current in both my covers and graphics.

To my beta readers for giving the books an early read.

To my proofreader, Latisha Rich, for the extra set of eyes.

To my fans, for the continued support.

Lastly, to my "writing voices," thank you for all the incredible ideas!

In loving memory of Jan Coulter.

Chapter One

The hushed tones of unearthly whispers pulled Jerry from sleep. He opened his eyes, saw it was still dark and closed them once more. Lying in the dark, he strained to decipher the words being said, but it was no use. Try as he might, the ghostly whispers were unclear to him.

He opened his eyes and saw Gunter crouched across the foot of the bed, intently staring toward the sitting area of the hotel suite. That Gunter hadn't alerted him to his visitors let him know they weren't a threat.

Jerry eased himself onto his elbow and spoke to his ghostly K-9 partner using only the power of his mind. *You're taking this whole watchdog thing too literally. I thought I told you not to let anyone in the room. That means actually doing something if anyone, living or dead, tries to come in.*

Gunter gave a low growl and continued to stare off in the distance.

Jerry heaved a sigh as he sat up and waited for his eyes to adjust to the dim lighting. He glanced at the clock: just after four in the morning. Not bad, considering he'd been in bed since nine the evening before in hopes of getting an early start to the day. He scanned the room, his gaze landing on two ghostly figures sitting on the sofa then trailing to his handgun lying on the nightstand next to the bed. *That won't do you any good, McNeal.* Not that he was worried. Had the visitors been of this realm, they never would have made it past the door without Gunter alerting him. Gunter might not have stopped the spirits from joining them, but Jerry never feared for his safety as long as his new companion was nearby.

Rising from the bed, he walked past his visitors without acknowledging them. Gunter followed.

"Good morning," a woman's voice called as he passed.

Jerry held up a finger. The spirits could wait; his bladder could not. Gunter saw where he was going and positioned himself between Jerry and the visitors.

Necessities completed, Jerry returned to the room, flipped up the light switch and squinted against the brightness, relieved to see that the two apparitions were spirits he'd encountered within the last couple of days. Why they were together he hadn't a clue, as the entities were as different as night and day. One was a quiet gentleman wearing a white cowboy hat, the other the spunky spirit of an older woman who wanted something from him but had somehow managed to forget what that something was.

While the man in the white hat had yet to reveal his identity, Jerry had seen what looked like a tin star pinned to the man's chest during a previous encounter. Jerry had a strong feeling he was the spirit of a Texas Ranger. Unfortunately, the spirit had disappeared before he had a chance to ask him, so what the lawman wanted from him remained unclear.

Jerry had tried multiple times to get a lead on the woman's identity, but so far, the only thing that kept presenting itself were the initials E.B. Those initials and an image of the Easter bunny were two more clues to the woman's identity than the spirit herself had offered. Obviously, she wasn't the Easter bunny, as she didn't have long ears or a cotton tail, but that was the image that kept coming to mind. Then again, it was probably because her petal-pink hair, bright blue eyelids, and brilliant pink lipstick reminded him of an Easter egg.

What they did have in common was that both had followed him to Deadwood. He'd seen the lawman hitchhiking on multiple occasions during his drive cross-country and once stopped to offer him a ride, only to have the guy respond, saying that Jerry was going the wrong way. The woman had taken more of a direct route, haunting a family that was on their way to Deadwood. Why she was looking for him, how she'd met the family or known Jerry would be there remained a mystery. Aside from his own deductions, the only thing he'd ascertained was neither spirit had anything to do with the case that had taken him to Deadwood. The only common thread in the mystery thus far was that both spirits seemed pleased to learn he would be heading to Texas for his next assignment.

Gunter plastered himself against Jerry's left leg as he stepped in front of the couch. Jerry wasn't sure if Gunter thought he needed him or if the dog merely wished to be involved in the questioning. Jerry looked from one spirit to the next. "I assume there's a reason you two are in my room."

The woman smiled at Gunter, then peered up at Jerry with a wide fuchsia grin. As she opened her brightly painted mouth, the man with the hat cut her off.

He narrowed his eye at Gunter before palming his hat and pointing it toward Jerry. "You're in the presence of a lady. I'd be most obliged if you'd do the respectable thing and cover yourself."

The woman's smile disappeared as her gaze settled on Jerry's briefs.

Jerry couldn't decide if she was disappointed that the man had insisted he put on pants or if she'd just realized his state of undress. Not that he cared either way – it was his room, and they were the ones invading his privacy. He started to tell the man the "lady" he was speaking of had appeared in his room on a previous occasion without concern for her virtue, and to assure him that she was safe from advances in any case. That the lawman's face lacked any hint of a smile told him arguing the point would be fruitless. Deciding to avoid conflict, he walked to the other side of the room to retrieve the jeans and shirt he'd placed in the chair the evening prior.

Jerry took his time getting dressed while Gunter remained seated in front of the couch, watching their ghostly visitors.

"I guess that's why they coined the term 'watchdogs.' All they do is watch," Jerry said as he pulled on his shoes. His remark was met with a lazy growl, which provoked a scowl from the ranger.

The woman waved a hand at Gunter. "Oh, poo, you don't scare me." She lifted her gaze to Jerry. "You said you were leaving today. We didn't want to miss our ride."

"You could have waited in my Durango," Jerry said tersely.

"We tried." She placed her hand in her lap and shifted in her seat. "There was a problem."

Jerry glanced toward the door. "There's a

problem with the Durango?"

The woman looked at the spirit sitting beside her and crossed her arms. "More of a problem with the seating arrangements."

Jerry raised an eyebrow. "I'm not following you."

"I want to sit in the front, but he told me I can't because he wants to sit there."

Jerry couldn't believe his ears. "You're telling me that you woke me at four in the morning squabbling about your seating arrangements like a couple of four-year-olds?"

The man pulled himself taller. "I assure you I am not one to squabble. I merely told the woman the way of it."

Don't do it, McNeal. Nothing good will come of it. "What way is that?"

"That women are to ride in the backseat while we menfolk tend to business."

"Why of all the nerve!" the woman huffed. "I have as much right to ride in the front seat as he does. Tell him, Jerry."

Jerry ran his hand over his head and addressed the woman. "Have you remembered your name yet?"

She wrung her hands together. "No, but it is on the tip of my tongue. I can feel it."

Jerry decided to take a chance. "Do the letters 'EB' sound familiar?"

The womanly spirit shook her head. "Maybe…I don't know."

Don't say it, Jer. "I'm also getting an image of a rabbit."

The gentleman spirit snickered and covered the sound with a cough. He squared his shoulders and looked Jerry in the eye. "I'd hoped you were a better detective than that."

Jerry took in the man's attire. "Given the star and the white hat, I'd say you're a Texas Ranger. It's too early in the morning for games. Perhaps you could just tell me your name?"

The man smiled. "Maybe I was too quick with my assumption. Clive Tisdale, Texas Ranger at your service."

At my service? What is that supposed to mean? "How can I help you, Mr. Tisdale?"

"I'd rather not say at the moment." Tisdale gave the slightest of nods to the woman sitting beside him. "It's a law matter."

"Ohhh, tell me. I love a good mystery. I've always been good at solving puzzles." Her face scrunched, and she scratched her head. "At least, I think I have."

Jerry started to point out that she couldn't even remember her own name when Clive intervened.

"Madam, I think your energy would be better spent trying to figure out why you are here and just what it is you want from this young man. If you spend all your time on the wrong puzzle, you may never get the answers you seek."

The woman bobbed her head and disappeared.

Tisdale cracked a smile. "Slightly more diplomatic than what you were thinking, was it not?"

Jerry chided himself for not blocking the spirit from gleaning his thoughts and quickly corrected the situation.

Tisdale's smile morphed into a chuckle. "No need to berate yourself. I would've known what you were thinking even if I hadn't read your mind. I've always been good at reading a fellow. That, and we rangers are trained in diplomacy. Better to talk a man down than to come out guns blazing."

Jerry moved to sit in a vacant chair. "What can I do for you, Mr. Tisdale?"

"Just Tisdale, or Clive if you'd prefer."

Jerry nodded. "What can I do for you, Clive?"

Tisdale leaned forward. As he did, Jerry's cell rang, the ring tone announcing Fred's call. Jerry shrugged his apologies as he answered his boss's call. "I'm awake. I've got something to tend to, then I'll be getting on the road."

"Good deal. Are you ready for the details, or do you want me to wait until after you've had your coffee?"

"I've got company. How about an abbreviated version for now?"

"Does the name Antonio Maioriello mean

anything to you?"

Jerry searched his mind. "No, should it?"

"Only if you've watched the news anytime within the last five years. The guy's a real tool. He makes Mario Fabel look like a choir boy. Five years back, he was nabbed. I'll spare you the ugly details for now and just say that, while being questioned, the man had an epiphany and decided to sing. He gave us enough to lock up half of Chicago. It was pretty big news. I'm surprised you never heard of it."

"It may come as a surprise to you, but I don't watch much television. I'm assuming the guy went into WITSEC. What does that have to do with me?"

"He did. Not long after the man entered the program, Maioriello and the Texas Ranger that had been babysitting him went missing without a trace, and the whole case fell apart."

At the mention of the Texas Ranger, Jerry's neck began to tingle. Perhaps it was because he just happened to have the spirit of a Texas Ranger sitting across from him. *It can't be a coincidence.* "So the government thinks they're dead?"

"They did until Maioriello turned up in photographs taken by the niece of Bruno Deluca, one of the men he rolled over on."

"Maioriello and this girl have a thing going on that they didn't disclose?"

"Not likely, since the man's three times older than her and has a face that can stop a train," Fred retorted.

"Perhaps the girl has a beef with her family, and this is her way of getting back at dear old dad," Jerry reasoned.

"All angles we've explored at great lengths. The girl works at the Alamo and had some friends in town. The four of them were hitting all the tourist attractions, and Maioriello showed up in almost all of their photos. She swears up and down she doesn't know how the guy made his way into the photos."

"Maybe someone doctored the photos after she took the pictures. It is amazing what people can do with Photoshop these days."

"She swears the camera never left her sight. We had a team look into their authenticity. Every theory has already been debunked."

Jerry wasn't convinced. "How so?"

"Because he also turned up in photos the girl didn't take herself. She has photographs taken from different places around San Antonio that offer tourists memorable pictures of their time at the attraction."

Jerry laughed. "She saw there was someone else in the photo and paid for the photos anyway?"

"Unlike you, she recognized the guy. She thought someone was messing with her and sent them to daddy."

"What'd daddy say?"

"He sent some of his people to have a talk with

the photographers and raised the bounty on Maioriello's head. And that is all we know about. This guy wants payback, and he's threatened the lives of the family of the Texas Ranger who was last assigned to his case."

"That ranger, his name wouldn't happen to be Clive Tisdale, would it?" Not likely, given Jerry's visitor looked to be from a different decade, but it was worth a shot.

"Not even close. The man's name is Raymond Hale. Why do you ask?"

"Because Clive Tisdale is sitting on the sofa in my hotel room."

"And he's a Texas Ranger?"

"Used to be."

"You're telling me that I'm calling you to investigate a case involving a Texas Ranger, and you just happen to have the spirit of a Texas Ranger sitting in the hotel room with you? He is a ghost, right?"

"Spirit, and yes."

"This has to be more than a coincidence," Fred said, reading Jerry's thoughts. "Did he give you anything?"

Jerry eyed Tisdale. "We'd just started our discussion when you called."

"Find out if he can shed some light on things and get back to me."

That Fred never once questioned Jerry's sincerity

spoke volumes. "Will do."

"You understand that my boss wants answers. If Maioriello is alive, you're to bring him to us."

Tisdale took this moment to draw a line across his throat.

Jerry sighed. "Maioriello's dead. Can I go home now?"

"How do you know?"

"You do know who you're talking to, right?"

"That's why you're on the case. We're going to need proof to shut Bruno down."

"And you think this Bruno guy is going to take my word for it?"

"Not a chance, but you've proven you have a way of convincing people you're telling the truth." Fred ended the call without waiting for a reply.

Jerry pocketed his cell phone and turned his attention to Tisdale. "I've got a case involving a missing Texas Ranger. I think it's safe to assume your being here is not a coincidence."

The corners of Tisdale's mouth lifted, and the hair on Jerry's neck began to crawl.

Gunter moved to Jerry's side, hackles raised.

Tisdale's smile waned. "Call off your mutt."

Jerry reached his hand to Gunter, who instantly eased his stance but kept staring at the man. Jerry wondered at the dog's actions. It wasn't like Gunter to be on alert when there wasn't a threat. And as far as he could tell, there wasn't one. He ran a hand along his ghostly partner's back to soothe him. "Easy, boy."

Tisdale's smile returned. "Never been a dog man myself. I find horses much more trustworthy."

"Yeah, well, a horse wouldn't fit in the Durango. Besides, I'm rather fond of the dog," Jerry added when Gunter grumbled.

Chapter Two

Jerry left his room just after six. Gunter moved to his left side while Clive Tisdale ambled close behind. The trio walked down the long hallway. Devoid of hotel guests, the hallway was anything but quiet due to the annoying tapping sound that echoed throughout the corridor. The sound was only audible to the three of them as far as Jerry could tell, as no one was investigating the noise. It was the spirit of Benjamin Worthington, an age-old miner he'd encountered in the hallway previously; of that, Jerry was sure. What he wasn't sure of was why he could now hear the taps from the hammer when he hadn't heard them the day before. Jerry kept his voice low so as not to disturb sleeping guests. "Benjamin is at it early."

Tisdale moved up to his side. "Benjamin?"

Jerry nodded. "Benjamin Worthington. He's

been mining a claim on this property for over a hundred years."

"Persistent fellow," Tisdale offered.

Jerry waited for Tisdale to say more, but he dropped back and continued to follow without another word. That was one thing he liked about the guy: unlike some spirits he'd encountered over the years, the man didn't seem to feel the need to talk just for the sake of filling the silence.

They rounded the corner, and just as Jerry suspected, Benjamin stood just outside the elevator hammering away at the gold-plated door, wearing the same faded red flannel shirt, suspendered pants and mud-caked shoes as before. The only thing missing was the donkey that had previously accompanied him.

"Any luck?" Jerry asked as he neared.

"Not today." Benjamin stopped what he was doing, his gaze taking in Jerry's two ghostly companions before traveling to the bag in Jerry's hand. "Looks like you'll be leaving us with one more than you arrived with."

Jerry smiled. "Yes, sir."

Gunter moved forward and boldly appraised Benjamin before moving to the elevator and sniffing at the base. The dog was so focused on what he was doing that Jerry wondered if Matilda, the man's donkey, was inside.

Benjamin frowned at Gunter, then took out a

handkerchief and used it to wipe his brow. "Be off with you, dog, afore you get yourself kicked in the chops."

Gunter ignored him briefly then moved to sniff the ground near Benjamin's feet. Growing bored with this, he moved in for a more personal examination. Gunter growled a low growl.

"I don't get many visitors up this way," Benjamin said, sidestepping Gunter's advances. He dropped his arm, positioning the pick in front of his crotch.

Jerry pretended to be waiting for the elevator as he and his ghostly entourage stopped to watch a man wearing cutoff shorts make his way past with two paper cups of rich-smelling coffee.

Jerry's mouth watered.

Benjamin inhaled, obviously enjoying the bold aroma. He closed his eyes for a long moment then opened them once more. "Most of the people I see are like that fellow, walking by without so much as a hello. He had two cups and never bothered to offer to share. Then there are those that step out of that hole right there and walk right through a fellow without so much as a backward glance. It's a rare day that someone such as yourself shows up and actually takes a moment to shoot the breeze. Why, that fellow beside you hasn't even had the decency to introduce himself, and I know he can see me."

Tisdale took that moment to join the

conversation. "I would have, only I didn't know if you knew you were dead."

Benjamin's mouth twitched. "Of course, I know. I'm not dense."

"Then why are you still here hammering away at a door, making enough racket to give a man a headache? That door is no more real than you are."

Benjamin smiled a sheepish grin. "Some habits are hard to break. Besides, it's not like everyone can hear me. And what else would you have me do? Follow this man around like the two of you are doing? Why are they following you in the first place?" he asked, turning his attention to Jerry.

Jerry shrugged. "It happens." Benjamin looked Tisdale up and down and for a moment, Jerry was afraid the man would ask to tag along.

The elevator dinged and the doors slid open.

Gunter leaned forward, craning his head and sniffing without stepping inside.

Jerry scanned the box but didn't see what had captured the dog's interest.

Benjamin stepped inside. As the doors slid shut, the bray of a donkey echoed from within.

Tisdale stepped up beside Jerry and scratched his head. "Peculiar fellow, don't you think?"

Jerry shifted his bag to the other hand and began walking again without replying. Why was it all spirits thought themselves normal and other entities to be an abnormality?

A middle-aged woman sat at the front desk. Eyes closed, her dark hair hung loose about her face. She opened her eyes just as Jerry neared, her cheeks turning a brilliant shade of pink at being caught sleeping on the job. She yawned and hurried to cover her mouth. "I'm so sorry. Being this tired at the beginning of my day doesn't bode well. I'm on my second cup of coffee, and it hasn't helped one single bit. If I wasn't the one to make the coffee, I'd think someone slipped decaf into the pot."

"Happens to the best of us," Jerry said louder than necessary, drawing the woman's attention as Gunter slipped behind the desk. The problem wasn't with the woman's lack of caffeine. It was that Granny stood behind her, playing a soft tune on the violin. Though he knew his grandmother had never played the instrument when alive, she now slid the bow expertly along the strings of the violin, playing a delicate melody that somehow besieged the recesses of the clerk's mind in a bid to lull her to sleep.

Jerry slid the envelope with his room key across the counter, and debated telling her that all the coffee in the world wouldn't work under the current conditions. Before he had a chance, Gunter sat on his haunches, lifted his head, and joined the chorus. It was a good thing he was the only one privy to actually hearing the ghostly duet, as they were making enough noise between the two of them to wake the dead. He cleared his throat to get his grandmother's attention.

Granny smiled and continued to play as she joined Jerry at the front of the desk. She swayed back and forth in an effort to avoid Gunter, who now greeted her with eager whines. Determined to finish her song, Granny slid the bow over the strings several more times before finishing with an ill-placed squeak.

The desk clerk's eyes grew wide as she looked directly at Granny. "Did you hear that?"

Jerry followed her gaze. "You mean the ghost playing the violin?"

The clerk cocked her head, looking at him as if he had two heads as she reached to pull his receipt from the printer. "And I thought I was in bad shape. I was talking about the noise coming from the casino. Sounds like someone just hit a nice jackpot. You know…checkout isn't until eleven. You might want to sleep it off a bit before you hit the road."

Jerry took the receipt from her hand. "I'm not drunk. I took the ghost walk last night. I guess my imagination is getting the better of me."

The clerk waved him off. "No worries. You're not the first person to come to Deadwood and think they heard a ghost." The clerk leaned in and lowered her voice. "They're not all made-up stories, you know. I've seen a few ghosts hanging around town. I'm gifted that way."

Tisdale chuckled as he passed a hand in front of the woman's unflinching face before moving past them and walking through the main entrance without bothering to open the door.

Jerry smiled at the woman. "Have a good day, ma'am."

"You too, Hun," the clerk said, settling back into her chair.

As Jerry turned, Granny tucked her hand through the crook of his arm, her touch as real as when the woman had lived. "When did you learn to play the violin?" he asked, keeping his voice low.

"Just this morning. I had to do something with that old fool making all the noise by the elevator."

That very fact had been bugging him. "Why is that? When I came in the other day, he was banging at the elevator, but I never heard a sound. I wonder what changed."

Granny's energy wavered. Instantly, Jerry knew she was to blame. "Why do I suddenly get the feeling you had something to do with the noise?"

"I guess I did," she said without apology. "The old geezer made a pass at me. I told him his hammer was so flat, he couldn't…"

Jerry shuddered. "Never mind! I don't want to know the details."

"Anyway, after I said what I said, he said he'd show me what his hammer could do, and he's been banging away at the door ever since."

Jerry struggled with his sense of duty to protect his grandmother's honor. He liked the old dude, but this was his grandmother. Still, even if he confronted the man, all the guy would have to do was disappear until Jerry got tired of waiting for him.

Gunter pressed into Jerry's leg as if to remind him he was there.

Jerry smiled. "Maybe I should send Gunter to have a word with the guy. What do you think, boy?"

Gunter woofed his readiness.

"You two behave. We all know I can take care of myself." She started walking, pulling Jerry along with her. "So, tell me, who's your gentleman friend?"

The question caught him off guard. "You don't know?"

Granny laughed a robust laugh. "Jerry McNeal, do you know every Marine on the planet?"

"No."

"Then what makes you think I should know every spirit that walks the earth?"

"I guess I just thought..."

"You should be ashamed of yourself. How many times have you gotten aggravated when someone assumed that you know the winning lottery numbers just because you are psychic? Or that you automatically know everything that is going to happen before it happens?"

Granny was right. Both were pet peeves of his.

He smiled sheepishly. "I guess I just thought things would be easier in the afterlife."

"Meaning you want to have all the answers."

Jerry shrugged. "Doesn't everyone?"

"The human mind craves knowledge. If you stop feeding it, then it withers and dies. Stop searching for the easy button and just live your life. Now, who's your friend?"

"His name is Clive Tisdale. He used to be a Texas Ranger. I think he has something to do with my next assignment."

Granny clicked her tongue. "You think he stopped being a ranger just because he's dead?"

Jerry stopped once more. "You see, that's what I don't get. Why must people have jobs in the afterlife?"

"Not people, Jerry, spirits." Granny hesitated as if considering her words. Finally, she continued. "We are free to do as we wish. Some move on to new things, others continue doing what they did before they left the world."

"Why?"

She shrugged. "Maybe they enjoyed it. Perhaps they feel they left things unfinished. Maybe they don't think anyone else can do whatever it is as good as them."

"This is all so convoluted. Why don't you have a job?"

"Who says I don't?"

"Do you?"

Granny patted his hand. "My job is the same as it always was."

"Which is?"

"Looking after you, Jerry." She began walking once more.

Not having another option, since her arm was still linked through his, Jerry followed. "Sounds like you got the short end of the stick, but I can't say I'm not glad."

She squeezed his arm gently. "I got exactly what I asked for and then some. I not only get to look after you, but now I get to spend time with your family. I love Max and April. I'm as blessed in death as I was when alive."

Gunter moved closer to his leg and gave a low woof.

Jerry ran his hand along the shepherd's back. "I'm happy to have you too, boy."

Granny stopped at the Durango. She peered through the window to see Tisdale sitting in the front seat and sighed.

"I can ask him to sit in the back," Jerry offered.

"No, you two have work to do. Best you get to it. I'm just disappointed you haven't taken my advice."

"Advice?"

"To slow down and take time to enjoy the sights. Here you are leaving, and you barely saw what the town has to offer."

Granny was right. Other than visiting Mount Moriah Cemetery and mingling with spirits of Deadwood's past on Main Street, he was once again guilty of leaving without exploring all the area had to offer. Even the ghost tour was a lie. Well, partial lie – he had seen ghosts walking the town, just not likely the ones mentioned on the guided tour. "I promise to see more of what the world has to offer."

Granny raised an eyebrow. "Good plan, except for one thing."

Jerry followed her gaze to Tisdale and knew he was the one thing she was referring to. "Are you sure you don't want to come along?"

Granny shook her head. "Can't. April's taking Max to get her ears pierced today, and I promised Max I would go with her and hold her hand so her mom doesn't see how nervous she is."

"She doesn't want it done?"

"Of course she does. She's the one who's been begging April to allow her to do it. That doesn't take away the whole needle in the ear thing." Granny looked at the back of her wrist. "Take the western route toward Denver."

"Dare I ask why?"

"The scenery is better."

Jerry frowned. "Isn't that out of my way?"

"Only by a few moments if you don't stop."

Jerry met her eye. "But I will be stopping, won't I?"

She looked at her wrist once more. "Time to go."

"You do realize you're not actually wearing a watch, right?"

"That's not all I'm not wearing." Granny disappeared in a wave of laughter as Jerry worked his way into a full-body shudder.

Chapter Three

"So why are you here, and what does your being here have to do with my going to Texas?" Jerry asked the moment he climbed inside the SUV.

"I'm here because you offered me a ride," Tisdale replied.

"I thought you were a straight shooter. Since when did you become a comedian?"

"I'm dead serious." Tisdale faded in and out as if to prove his point.

"Very funny." Jerry pushed the start button on the Durango, and the Hemi engine rumbled to life. He started to tell the man to buckle his seatbelt and caught himself.

Tisdale worked his fingers across the dashboard, pushing buttons and leaning forward to inspect his handiwork. "You'll find out in due time."

Jerry resisted the urge to push his hand away.

Instead, he reset everything to his liking. "It doesn't work that way. You were ready to tell me before my boss called. Why get close-lipped all of a sudden?"

Tisdale powered down the passenger window. "Your boss told you enough for the time being. Besides, my job isn't to solve your case for you."

Jerry sighed. "Have you been talking to my grandmother?"

"The woman playing the violin? No, I haven't had the pleasure. She seems like a lively spirit. Reminds me of a woman I had the pleasure of knowing back in the day. Why, that woman could…"

Jerry raised the man's window using the buttons on the driver's side door. "Stop touching things, or I'll make you switch places with the dog."

Tisdale placed his hands in his lap and looked straight ahead without another word. Jerry decided the silence to be better than having Tisdale regale him with details, thus placing unwanted images in his head.

***

Tisdale lowered the window on the passenger side of the SUV for at least the twentieth time since leaving Deadwood. They'd been on the road for three hours, and the spirit had yet to give Jerry a straight answer about why he was here.

Jerry felt he'd shown extreme patience with the man, but that patience was fast wearing thin as the wind rushing in caused a deafening roar in his ears.

Jerry used the button on his left hand side to raise the window. "The air's on," Jerry said as Tisdale's hand returned to the button.

Tisdale drummed his finger on the lever, trying to lower the window. "The air is outside."

"The air conditioning," Jerry corrected. He pointed to the dash. "If you're hot or cold, you can use that button to adjust the temperature on your side. Only that one; don't touch anything else," Jerry said when Tisdale reached for the dash.

Tisdale jerked his hand back. "I'm neither. I just want to feel the air in my face."

Jerry thumbed his hand over his shoulder to where Gunter stood in the backseat with his head sticking through the glass pane. "Then do what he's doing."

Tisdale craned his neck to see and turned around with a huff. "I assure you I am much too civilized for that."

Jerry leaned over and adjusted the vent. "Better?"

"I'd be better if I was on my horse."

Jerry patted the dash. "We have the power of 360 horses right here."

Gunter pulled his head inside and woofed from his spot in the backseat. Jerry glanced in the mirror, and Gunter dipped his head over the seat, smiling a K-9 smile.

Tisdale batted him away, and Gunter growled a

grumbling growl.

Jerry sighed and leaned into the back of his seat. "If you two don't learn to get along, this is going to be a long trip."

Tisdale ignored him. "I was a horse man myself. Never had much use for dogs."

This evoked a full snarl from Gunter.

"A horse wouldn't fit in the seat." Jerry glanced in the mirror, winking at Gunter.

"In my day, all a man needed was a rifle, sturdy horse, and comfortable saddle."

Jerry pointed a finger toward the dash. "According to the navigator, it's one thousand, two hundred and forty miles to San Antonio. How many miles could you ride in a day?"

"Depends on the terrain and the weather conditions," Tisdale replied.

Jerry slid a glance in the man's direction. "Come on, give me a ballpark?"

Tisdale raised an eyebrow. "A what?"

"Give me a rough estimate of how many miles a horse could travel in a single day," Jerry said, rephrasing the question.

"I guess ten to twenty."

"Okay, for the sake of argument, let's say you have a fast horse that would let you ride fifty miles a day."

Tisdale blew out a long whistle. "Yep, that'd be some horse, alright."

"Then let's say you could manage sitting in the saddle that long. It would take you twenty-five days of hard riding to get where we're going." Jerry gave Tisdale a hard look. "We could be there tomorrow night, but since this is not a matter of national security, I plan on stopping for the night and sleeping in a real bed. Even so, we will be there the day after tomorrow."

Tisdale furrowed his brow. "I guess I can see the merits of driving this beast. But I have to ask, where do you keep your shotgun? I understand there is room in the back, but you'd have to stop and get out of the vehicle to make use of it."

Jerry started to tell the man this wasn't the Old West, and he'd likely never find himself in a situation where he would need to pull a shotgun, but he decided to have some fun instead. He pulled to the side of the road and pressed the button for the sunroof, watching as the covering slid back. Instead of exposing the sky, it gave way to an exceptional display of weapons, any of which he could get his hands on within seconds.

Tisdale's eyes bugged. "Are you expecting a war?"

Jerry smiled. "No, but if I were, I'd like to think I'd be ready for it."

Tisdale surveyed the overhead compartment. "I can see where that could come in handy."

"Better than a horse?" Jerry teased.

Tisdale shrugged. "Depends on the horse. Horses are not only for travel. Why, a good horse will let you know when something's afoot."

Gunter snorted.

"Don't go getting all riled. I know dogs can do that too, but dogs are more inclined to stand there and fight to the death than to carry you away from the fight. I had this one mare that would do just that. Laura Bell was her name, named after a fiery lass with raven hair as dark as the horse." Tisdale sighed. "That's a story for another time. Anyhow, there was this one time I was hunting this fellow, and it wasn't long before I realized he'd turned the tide and was now following me. He was an ornery cuss accused of killing nine men. I wasn't inclined to be the tenth, so I knew I had to keep my wits about me so the fellow didn't get the upper hand. I ate a cold meal of jerky and wild onion, plus I'd come upon a farmer earlier in the day who'd given me a bit of bread. I flicked off the weevils. I'd have eaten them too if not for having the jerky to fill my belly that day. I only had that because I traded another farmer a fresh-killed deer for enough jerky to fill my sack. While I ate, Laura Bell refused to settle. She reacted to every little noise, and so I knew something was afoot. I hadn't slept much the day before and knew I needed a few winks just to keep my wits about me. I kept Laura Bell's saddle on her and packed everything away, including my bedroll. I gave her enough rein so she could move about while I slept and wrapped the end of the tether around my hand. Sometime during the night, she stirred and pulled hard at the tether, giving me my cue. I was on her back in an instant, trusting her to carry me away from danger. Horses are more likely to flee danger than dogs, don't you think?"

Though Tisdale had a valid point, Jerry knew he wasn't seeing the whole picture. "Would your horse take a bullet for you?"

"I've had several good horses shot out from under me."

Jerry shook his head. "That's not what I'm talking about. I'm asking you if your horse would purposely put herself between you and a bullet. Say that man who was following you snuck up on you while you were sleeping."

Tisdale cut him off. "He wouldn't, because my horse would know him to be there."

"Okay, let's say the horse didn't, and this man snuck up on you."

Tisdale sat up in the seat and crossed his arms. "I can't say that because it wouldn't happen."

Great, the guy's willing to accept a horse traveling fifty miles a day, but not one that allows for an ambush. Think, McNeal. "Okay, this guy is already with you and decides to shoot you."

"Why would he want to shoot me?"

Gunter emitted a groan from the backseat, and

Jerry resisted the urge to laugh. "He's a bad guy, and he wants you dead."

"I'm assuming I have previously captured the rascal. I don't take my job lightly, so where'd he get the gun?" Tisdale asked tersely.

Jerry lifted his hand, intending to give Tisdale a whack on the back of his head, but ran it over his own head instead. "Let's say for the sake of argument that you come upon a total stranger on a lonely trail. It's late, you're tired, and this guy is cooking a stew that smells so good, you can smell it from the back of your horse. Your stomach rumbles, and this guy hears it."

"He must have good hearing if I'm on the back of my horse and he's standing over a cooking pot."

"I didn't say he was...okay, the man has exceptional hearing. He hears your stomach and invites you to have supper with him. He looks like a nice guy, so you agree. You give your horse a rest and sit to have a meal with the man. While eating, the two of you talk, and you tell him you're a lawman. Now, this guy has just killed a man a few days back, and he gets all scared thinking you have come looking for him."

Tisdale cut him off. "You know, for a fellow with exceptional hearing, the guy's not very bright. If he's on the run from the law, he shouldn't have stopped long enough to cook a stew, nor should he have invited a stranger to eat it with him."

Jerry gripped the wheel tighter in an attempt to control his frustration. "Yep, he's the dumbest criminal there is, and now he wants to do something even dumber, which is to shoot a lawman. He pulls the gun and gets the drop on you. What is that horse of yours doing?"

"Depends."

Jerry shot him a glance. "What do you mean 'depends'?"

"Just what I said. If it's a hot night, she's probably using her tail to bat away the flies. If it is a cold night…"

Oh, for the love of … "Anywhere! Anywhere at all in this scenario, does your horse know anything is wrong?"

"No, I doubt she does."

"So, she wouldn't come rushing over and put herself between you and the bad guy?"

"Of course not. There's a fire and horses don't like fires."

Finally! "See that dog in the backseat? He died protecting his partner, who was facing a man with a gun. Without any thought of his own life, Gunter dove in front of the man, giving his partner just enough time to take aim and save himself from sure death. That guy is still on the job and owes his life to this dog. You won't see a horse doing that. I don't care how well it is trained. That's why dogs are man's best friend. They are willing to give their life

34

to save them. So don't go giving me this horses are better BS, because it isn't going to fly. You give me a choice between a horse and a dog, I'll take the dog!"

Gunter woofed his approval.

Tisdale turned and tipped his hat in the dog's direction. "Well done, sir."

Jerry glanced in the mirror just in time to see Gunter smile.

"Why you?" Tisdale asked, drawing Jerry's attention.

"Why me what?"

"You said that guy, so you obviously weren't talking about yourself. Why is the dog with you and not with his old partner?"

Jerry debated his answer and then decided to answer with a question of his own. "Why are you here with me and not on that horse you're so fond of?"

Tisdale smiled. "Well played, sir. Well played."

Jerry was glad his answer appeased the man, as the only other explanation he had was that he needed the dog and couldn't imagine his life without him.

Chapter Four

Jerry knew the phone was going to ring even before the Durango's dash lit up, alerting him of April's call. The instant he pushed the button to connect, he also knew something was wrong.

He gripped the steering wheel, trying not to allow his imagination to get the better of him. "Are you and Max alright?"

April's sigh was audible. "I'm never going to be able to keep anything from you, am I?"

"I hope you never feel the need to," Jerry said, relaxing ever so slightly. "Now, what's bothering you, and how can I make it right?"

Tisdale chuckled. "I never had you pegged for a Casanova."

"I'm not a Casanova."

"Where'd that come from? You know I trust you, don't you?"

Jerry closed his eyes for the briefest of moments. "I wasn't talking to you. I was talking to Tisdale."

"Tisdale? Is he the man in the white hat?"

It was clear that he, too, would not be able to keep anything from those he loved. "Let me guess, Max told you."

"She did. She also said your lady friend paid you another visit."

"My lady friend? Oh, the Easter bunny."

"Your lady friend is a rabbit?"

Instantly, Jerry was reminded of the movie *Harvey* with Jimmy Stewart. A classic, he and his grandmother had watched it over a dozen times. "No, but it would make it a lot more interesting if she was. As it is, the woman doesn't have a clue what her name is."

"So, you call her the Easter bunny? That doesn't seem very nice."

"No, at least not to her face."

"I'm pretty sure you did," Tisdale said, adding fuel to the flame.

Jerry looked at the man. "I'm not talking to you."

"Do you want me to let you go?" April's tone was light, showing she knew he was not talking to her.

"No! Don't hang up. Just give me a minute." He looked at Tisdale once more. "I would like to talk to my lady if you don't mind."

Tisdale shrugged. "Go ahead."

"Alone!" Jerry took a breath and lightened his tone. "Could you give us a few moments of privacy?"

Tisdale disappeared without a word.

Jerry rolled his neck. "Now, where were we?"

"Are we alone?"

Jerry looked in the mirror and locked eyes on Gunter. "Alone enough."

"Hi, Gunter," April said, understanding the comment.

Gunter woofed.

"Gunter says hello back."

"Where are you?"

That she was trying to change the subject wasn't lost on him. "In the Durango."

"Very funny."

"Just outside of Cheyenne, Wyoming. I should be passing through Denver in a couple of hours."

"Denver? That's close to Rocky Mountain National Park, right?"

"Not too far, yes."

"I saw on the news there is a big search going on over there."

Jerry peered at the dash. "What kind of search?"

April laughed. "You really have to start listening to the news more."

"I don't like the news. It's too depressing." That was the short of it; the long of it was each story set him off, wreaking havoc on his spidey senses. It was the same anytime he was in a large crowd, as his internal radar honed in on every minor conflict.

"For a man named Greg Oswald. He's a teacher and a girls' softball coach. Apparently, his team was set to play in the playoffs, and he went missing. They think he might be lost in the forest. Max has been crazy upset about it."

"What does Max have to do with this?"

"She didn't tell you? She's been working with Houdini to train him in search and rescue. She's been hiding things around the yard, and he seems to have a knack for finding them. I think it's good for him, as he's only chewed up one pair of flip-flops since you've been gone. Anyway, we've been watching search and rescue videos, and this one just showed up yesterday. I checked when I woke up and they've yet to find the guy. Max said if Houdini was trained, she would have Fred fly them there in the Learjet so they could help search for him. We'd better not tell her you're close or she'll insist you and Gunter join the search."

"She may already know."

"She hasn't mentioned it."

"Granny stopped me this morning and insisted I take the western route. Something about the scenery, which has been phenomenal, but I know she and Max have been spending a lot of time together, so that may have been what prompted it."

"Are you going to go?"

"I'm sure they have enough help."

"If the guy is still missing, then they don't have the right help," April said softly.

"Meaning a psychic?"

"I was thinking more of a ghost dog, but I guess you could help too."

"Ouch, cut me a little deeper."

April laughed. "I didn't mean anything by it, and you know it."

"I know, I was just messing with you. You said Max has watched the videos of this guy. She's usually good at picking up on things. Has she mentioned getting anything on him?"

"She said she sees a baseball bat. That's not anything new because he's been coaching for years, and they keep showing him with his softball team."

While it was possible, Jerry didn't think so. Max's psychic intuition was good, and she normally didn't pick up on things without a reason. He remembered how she helped with the Hash Mark Killer, and how her mentioning the bells was one thing that linked the victims together. "Don't discount the bat. It probably means something. Tell her to let me know if she gets anything else."

"Okay."

"I miss you. Max too. I'm looking forward to seeing you. Hello?" Jerry said when April didn't answer.

"I'm here."

"Come on, April, just rip the band-aid off. Whatever you have to say to me can't be that bad."

"I can't meet you in Texas. I want to, and I feel just awful."

Jerry worked to hide his disappointment. "Is there a problem?"

"It's the designer. He wants to meet with me to show me the plans and discuss some things."

"Pretty convenient since you're out of town," Tisdale's voice sang out, showing the man may have disappeared, but he was still listening in on the conversation.

Jerry lifted a finger to get Gunter's attention. The dog woofed and appeared in the front passenger seat, staring at Jerry with a satisfied grin.

Still, Tisdale's words haunted him. "Kind of convenient that Mr. Krieger waits until I'm away to want to go over the designs."

Laughter floated through the dash. "Jerry McNeal, I do believe you are jealous."

A little. "Only that he gets to spend time with you, and I don't."

"For your information, Mr. Krieger is old enough to be my dad." April's voice turned serious. "I can cancel if you want, but he's already told me he is working on several projects at once and will move one of the others in front if we can't settle things."

"What's the problem?"

"No problem, really. I just have to look things

over and make sure they are in the right place."

"And it can't be done via e-mail?"

"He's old school. Likes to meet face to face to show the changes and discuss things. It's your fault, you know."

"My fault? I'm barely involved with this. Not that I'm complaining, I've already told you I'm happy as long as the roof doesn't leak and the toilets flush."

"Yes, well, it was the addition of the safe room you insisted on having installed that threw things off."

"Some men want a man cave. I just want to see my family safe."

"And your family appreciates that, as long as we can figure out the best place to put it." April sighed. "There's one other thing."

Jerry glanced at the dash. "I'm listening."

"Max wants a pool."

"Okay."

April laughed. "It's not that easy. This is Michigan. You can only swim a few months out of the year."

"So put it inside."

"Now you sound like Max. Do you know what it would take to build a house with an indoor pool?"

"No, but I'd be willing to bet Mr. Krieger does."

"Jerry, that's a lot of money. Are you sure?"

"Yes, if it will make you and Max happy, it's

worth it."

"Me? Max is the one that wants the pool."

"Which you will use just as much as she does. And you will bear the brunt of her attitude if she doesn't get it."

"So, you're saying it's better to give in."

"I'm saying I missed out on the first thirteen years of her life, and if saying yes to a pool makes me Dad of the Year, I'm okay with that."

"You don't have to spend a lot of money on her for Max to adore you," April said in return.

"I know, but what good is having money if I can't spend it on the ones I love?"

"We love you, Jerry, with or without a pool. But maybe I'll take Max with me to meet Mr. Krieger. If she can help with the design, it will help take some of the sting away when I tell her we can't meet you in San Antonio."

"I wish I had something to take the sting away," Jerry said smoothly.

Gunter yawned a sorrowful yawn.

Jerry laughed, and April's voice floated through the speakers once more. "What's so funny?"

"I think Gunter just told us to get a room," Jerry replied.

"Hey, come back here with that!" April's words were followed by a string of near obscenities and heavy breathing. "Drop it!"

Jerry looked at Gunter. "I think your boy's in

trouble. You'd better do something, or she's going to trade him in on a poodle!"

Gunter disappeared.

"Give it back! Uh-oh, your dad's here. You're in trouble now. Ha, ha, thank you, Gunter."

"Everything okay?" Jerry asked when the dash grew quiet.

"It is now. Gunter saved the day. So much for Houdini being on his best behavior. That little stinkpot took off with my new bra."

Jerry pictured April running through the house topless in a desperate attempt to capture the dog and retrieve her undergarment. "That's my boy."

"You're such a guy!" April said, and Jerry could picture the eye-roll that went with the statement.

"You've discovered my one flaw."

"Oh, for pity's sake. No wonder the dog left," Tisdale said, reclaiming his seat.

"And for the record, I'm not running around topless. I was doing laundry," April informed him.

"So, just because I'm a guy, you assume my mind instantly went to the gutter?"

"Didn't it?"

Jerry smiled at the dash. "Guilty as charged. Is everything okay there now?"

"Yep, Gunter corralled him long enough for me to retrieve my bra. You may have lost your wingman for a while. They are now outside running the fence together."

"Good, maybe it will settle them both down."

"What's wrong with Gunter?"

"He and my current guest don't seem to get along." Jerry switched lanes to accommodate a semi coming off the on-ramp.

"I thought he only gets upset when there is a threat from the entity." April's voice was full of concern.

Jerry glanced at Tisdale. "I don't think he's a threat to anything but Gunter's ego. They both want the same thing."

"Which is?"

"To sit in the front seat," Jerry answered as he checked his mirror and returned to the right lane.

"Sounds like an interesting trip."

Jerry nodded his head. "To say the least. Listen, traffic is starting to get heavy. I'm going to get going for now."

"Okay, Jerry, I love you."

"I love you too, Ladybug." Jerry pressed the dash to end the call and gave Tisdale a glance. "Not a word."

Tisdale smiled. "What? I like ladybugs."

Chapter Five

Jerry replayed his and April's conversation multiple times, focusing on the part where she told him about the missing softball coach. The man had been missing, presumably in a forest with creatures more than capable of killing and eating him, for at least two days. That the rescuers hadn't found him meant he was either dead, moving around – thus impeding his chances of being found – or injured and unable to help searchers find him. Jerry concentrated on the man's name and what little he knew about the guy. *He doesn't feel dead. I'm already in the area, so why not take a look?*

"Because you already have an assignment. Or doesn't a sense of duty mean anything to you?"

"I thought I blocked you."

"You can't block your conscience."

Jerry slid a glance in Tisdale's direction. "The

last I checked, you were not my conscience."

"Obviously not, or you'd be listening to me instead of deciding to run off after a jackass."

"Jackass? That's pretty cold since you don't know if the guy's alive or dead." Jerry hesitated. "You don't, do you?"

"Of course not. But I do know the lay of the land and how to tell if I'm stumbling around or following the sun, moon, or stars to see my way home. The man's dumb enough to get himself lost in the forest, he can't be all that bright. Maybe we should just leave him to the wolves and coyotes."

Jerry decided to play on the man's sense of duty. "Who's to say he got lost? Maybe there's something more sinister at play."

"Sinister?"

Got ya. "Yes, maybe there was foul play. Don't you think that's worth a look-see?"

Tisdale shifted in his seat. "I suppose it wouldn't hurt to swing by and see for ourselves."

"I agree. And that is precisely why I intend on doing just that." It wasn't that he needed the spirit's permission; it was that getting permission was easier than listening to Tisdale's mouth the whole way. As he drove closer to the exit, his spidey senses took over, and Jerry knew it wasn't up to either of them. The feeling was so intense, he wouldn't have been able to pass without checking in to see if he could help. He took the exit to the Rocky Mountain

National Park and smiled at Tisdale. "Wait for it."

"Wait for w…"

The dash lit up even before Tisdale could finish his question. Jerry pushed the button on the dash, answering Fred's call. "What can I do for you, Mr. Jefferies?"

Fred chuckled. "You already did it."

"I'm not following you."

"No, you're following that gift of yours, and it earned me a C-note."

Jerry smiled. "Translated, you and Barney had a wager, and he's now out a hundred dollars."

"Bingo."

"Have you ever lost a bet to him?"

"Not unless we find out man didn't really walk on the moon."

"I thought with all your clearances, you'd already have the answer to that."

"Who says I don't? Maybe I just don't want to pay off the wager."

"Are you saying we didn't go to the moon?"

Fred laughed a hearty laugh. "Care to place a wager?"

"Nope," Jerry said, remembering his conversation with April. "I have a house and swimming pool to pay for."

"Smart man." Fred's voice turned serious. "The question is, did you get a pull, or have you broke your code and started listening to the news?"

"Max knew. April told me about it, and then I got the pull."

"Think the man's still alive?"

"I have a feeling he is, but not for long unless he's found."

"Want me to call ahead and let them know you're coming?"

Jerry thought about that for a moment. "No, let me go in and do what I do. They find out I'm coming, and it might change things."

"How so?"

"Either they will think I'm a fraud, or they will put all their eggs in my basket. Neither will help the guy. It's best to let me feel my way along and see where my spidey senses lead me." Jerry smiled an inward smile, knowing Seltzer would be proud that he'd come to grips with calling it that. "I have my badge and will let you know if I need anything."

"Roger that," Fred said and ended the call.

"I sure could have used one of those back in the day."

"One of what?"

"One of those telephones."

That Tisdale knew what the communication device was called let Jerry know the man's spirit had been walking the earth for some time. What he didn't know was if Tisdale had ever found anyone to help him before. "This can't be your first case since you passed."

Tisdale shook his head. "No, son, it's not."

"Have there been others like me?"

"Lawmen, yes. Lawmen who can actually see and hear me without my making a fuss about it, no. It makes things a whole lot easier, that's for sure."

"I suppose it would," Jerry agreed. "Do you enjoy being a Texas Ranger?"

Tisdale snorted. "Why, that's like asking a fellow if he likes breathing."

"Yes, I suppose it is." He waited for Tisdale to expound on the comment, but it wasn't to be. Jerry didn't mind, as the feeling pulled him forward and gave him something else to occupy his mind. He continued driving and followed the signs to the Rocky Mountain National Park, but even as he did, something felt off. Even as he pulled into the park and followed the road to the right, he rolled his shoulders and drummed his fingers on the steering wheel.

"What's on that mind of yours, son? You're as twitchy as a mare being harassed by a horsefly," Tisdale said at last.

"This is the way to the search," Jerry said, passing the turn-off to the visitors' center. "I can feel it. But something's not right. I feel like he's here, but he's not." He continued on US 36, following several vehicles up into the park, stopping when he came to the official entrance to the park marked by four lanes. The gate was down for the right lane, so Jerry followed a car into one of the adjoining lanes and idled behind as the car stopped at the check station. There were police cars blocking the road ahead just past the guardhouse. Armed uniformed officers stood beside their patrol cars as if daring anyone to pass. The car in front remained there for several moments before pulling forward, then circling in front of the officers and returning the way it had come.

Jerry brought his hand up, hiding the movement of his lips. "They're not letting anyone up."

"You should have let your boss clear the way," Tisdale said, echoing Jerry's inner thoughts.

Jerry pulled up to the guardhouse and was met with a no-nonsense stare from the woman inside. He placed his foot on the brake and wrestled his wallet out of the front pocket of his pants. He flashed his badge. "Jerry McNeal. They are expecting me up on the ridge."

"I'm sorry, sir, your name isn't on the list," the woman said, checking her clipboard. Jerry was about to argue when the woman looked in the rear window and smiled. "Oh, you're with the search dog group."

Jerry looked in the mirror to see Gunter had returned and was now sitting in the back seat wearing his K-9 police vest. He wondered if it was because Gunter knew they were on a mission or if it was simply to help him pass through the gates with ease. He turned his attention to the woman and smiled a disarming smile. "Yes, ma'am."

"I'm sorry, we've just had so many people coming to help with the search. It's getting late and they don't want to have to worry about anyone else getting lost in the woods. I sure hope you can help them find Coach Oswald. There are a lot of people praying for him." She handed him an orange tag. "They have patrols out dispatching the gawkers. Put that on your rearview mirror, and no one will stop you from going up the hill. The command center is set up by Deer Mountain. Just keep going straight, you can't miss it."

Jerry looped the card around the mirror and laid his wallet in the center console. "Thank you, ma'am."

"No, thank you. Now go find Coach."

"What's with the dog?" Tisdale asked as they pulled away.

"Gunter lets people see him when necessary."

Gunter growled then managed several eager yips.

"But…"

Jerry addressed Tisdale as he waited for the officer to back his car out of the way. "I'm tired of playing referee to the two of you. Get along or at least learn to deal with each other. I've got enough on my mind without running interference."

Tisdale pulled himself taller in the seat.

"Whatever you say. You're the boss."

That's more like it. Jerry stepped on the gas, enjoying the sound of the Durango's Hemi engine. He eased off the pedal to comply with the speed limit within the park, which after hours on the highway now felt as if he were backing up, and rolled his neck to relieve the tension as he followed the pull guiding him up the mountain and gaining in intensity with each turn of the wheel.

"That's some fine eating right there," Tisdale said, pointing out a small herd of elk.

Jerry took in the size of the elk, most of which were quadruple the size of a large deer, and decided the lower speeds were warranted. "I'd hate to hit one of those."

Tisdale jumped on his comment. "Wouldn't have to worry about hitting one if you were riding a horse."

"I wouldn't have to worry about you sitting beside me nagging me either," Jerry said dryly.

Tisdale looked over his shoulder and Gunter growled.

Jerry gripped the wheel to keep from losing his cool, then relaxed when he saw the tented command post looming ahead. The searchers may not have found the guy yet, but they were looking in the right area. Of that, he was sure. He parked behind a park ranger vehicle and took in the scene. There was a white tent with a half dozen people milling about.

Several news crews were positioned at the base of the hill as if doing so might give them the benefit of a first scoop.

Jerry got out of the SUV and started toward the tent. Gunter fell in beside him as Tisdale moved to his right side. Though Jerry had wrestled with his abilities over the years, he did not lack confidence. Still, with Gunter and Tisdale at his side, an image of Wyatt Earp walking toward the O.K. Corral with his brother Virgil and Doc Holiday came to mind, and suddenly, Jerry felt rather invincible.

A man wearing a lime-green reflector vest turned in his direction. His eyes narrowed as his lips drew together. He slammed the clipboard he was holding down on the table, causing several of those standing around him to flinch. He pointed a finger at Jerry. "Is that your dog?"

Jerry looked down at Gunter, who'd sidled up to his left side the moment he exited the Durango. He was about to claim ownership when the man pointed past him and spoke with more authority.

"Whose shepherd is that, and why isn't it on a leash?" the man bellowed.

Jerry turned, looked to where the man was pointing and felt the color drain from his face. Six months old, all legs and the mirror image of his ghostly canine father, minus the battle scars and missing piece of ear, Houdini was standing directly behind him. Wagging his tail, the gangly pup looked outrageously pleased with himself. Instantly, Jerry's mind went to the obvious, and he searched the area for Max and April. Not seeing them, he swallowed and whispered to Gunter, "How the devil did he get here?"

Gunter answered with a K-9 grin.

"Get that blasted dog on a leash!" the man yelled once more.

Gunter growled and Houdini's ears pitched forward as he barked and looked ready to join his father in battle.

Jerry held out his hand, praying the pup would heed the command. "Stay!"

"I tried to tell you there were two of them, but you wouldn't listen," Tisdale said, using his hat to hide the humor in his face. "Better put that pup on a leash before he raises that man's ire enough to get us all kicked out of here."

Jerry clapped his hand to his side. "Houdini, heel."

All feelings of being invincible left as the pup dipped into a bow, wagged his tail and looked at Jerry as if to ask, *Who put you in charge*?

Chapter Six

Jerry took a step toward Houdini. The pup broke his stance, circling and watching for Jerry to make his next move. Jerry held out his hand and Houdini stretched out his nose. Jerry reached for him, and the pup darted to the side. *Great, I'm here to help find a man who might be near death, and this guy wants to play.* Jerry didn't like not being in control of a situation. It certainly didn't help that everyone was watching. "Houdini!"

The pup stilled, ears erect, staring at him.

Jerry took a step forward.

Houdini was off like a shot, tongue hanging from his mouth, obviously enjoying the game.

Still wearing his police vest, Gunter yawned a squeaky yawn and looked at Jerry as if to say, *You're on your own. I have work to do.*

Jerry started to remind Gunter that he was the

one responsible for the pup being here in the first place but didn't get the chance, as the ghostly K-9 disappeared and reappeared just inside the open tent. He gave Jerry a long look, then turned, walking through the space nose to the ground.

Tisdale placed a hand on Jerry's shoulder. "You're not very good with animals, are you, son?"

Before Jerry could answer, his cell rang, sounding April's ringtone. Ignoring Tisdale's remark, he fished the phone from his pocket.

Tisdale smiled. "Bet you're rethinking that horse about now." He chuckled at his own statement, then he, too, headed toward the tent.

Jerry struggled to remain calm as he answered April's call. "Hello."

"Jerry, Houdini is missing," April sobbed.

Jerry glanced at the pup, who now stood twenty feet away, watching his every move.

"Maybe I should call Uncle Fred and see if he can help."

Uncle Fred? "Max?"

"Yes." Max sniffed.

"I thought you were your mom. You sounded just like her for a moment."

"No, it's me. I'm just using Mom's phone. Mine died and I have it charging." The distraction seemed to have calmed her. "Houdini's missing. Gunter too, but I figured he went back to you. I need to call Uncle Fred so he can send someone to help find him."

"NO! Don't call Fred." *Easy, McNeal. Don't take your frustrations out on the kid.* "Listen, Max, I don't know how, but Houdini is here. They both are."

"Houdini is with you?! Mom, Jerry said Houdini is with him! I don't know. Mom wants to talk to you."

There was a short silence, followed by muffled words, then April's voice floated through the phone. Though her voice had an edge, hearing it was just what he needed. Even when upset, April's voice was a beacon, a calming wind in an unpredictable storm. "How did Houdini get there, and why didn't you let us know? We've been looking for him for nearly twenty minutes."

"I don't know how he got here. I assume he followed Gunter."

"How is that even possible?" April pressed.

"I don't know, but it isn't the first time they've traveled together, so it's the only explanation."

"Traveled?"

"I'm not sure what else to call it." Jerry looked on as Gunter and Tisdale moved about the tent, stopping at each person in turn. No one seemed to notice their presence, and Jerry knew they were the perfect team, listening to conversations no one else could hear. Jerry envied their stealthy tactics and couldn't wait to be apprised of the information they gathered.

"We were so worried. I wish you would have told us," April said, drawing his attention.

"I just found out myself. Listen, this isn't a good time. I'm here at the search site. I need to get Houdini on a leash before they kick us out of here. I'm trying to catch him, but he isn't listening. Every time I take a step toward him, he runs."

"Did you give him a command?"

Jerry blew out a frustrated sigh. "Sort of. I called his name but didn't actually follow through with a command."

"Tell him to come."

"COME!" Houdini stared at him, unmoving. Jerry firmed his voice. "COME!"

Houdini lowered into a crouch.

"Are you alright, Jerry? I feel like something's off. You know how to handle him. You're the one who taught me."

It was true. The pup's appearance flustered him so much that he reacted instead of acting. He didn't usually have to worry about commands, not with Gunter anyway. For the most part, he only had to think about something, and Gunter would act on it. He was so caught up in the feeling and finding the man that Houdini's presence had nearly sent him into panic mode. April's call and the even tone in her voice helped rein him in. "I'm okay. I'm just not used to being tugged in the opposite direction when following the pull."

"I know." April's voice remained smooth and calm. "Don't yell at him. He's going to think he's in trouble."

"He already does." Jerry clapped his leg and eased his tone. "Houdini, come."

The transformation in the pup was instantaneous. Houdini sprang to his feet, tail wagging as he rushed to where Jerry stood. "It worked. Good boy, Houdini. Good, come."

April laughed once more. "It usually helps when he knows what you're asking of him, and if all else fails, open the door to the Durango and tell him you're going bye-bye. That'll get him every time."

"Good to know. Listen, I've got to go. I'll give you a call after I see what's going on here. Oh, and tell Max to let me know if she gets a hit on this guy."

"Okay, will do. Love you."

"Love you too." Jerry ended the call and pocketed his phone. "Houdini, heel."

Houdini sidled up to Jerry's left side, walking in step as he returned to the Durango. Jerry opened the door, smiling as Houdini jumped inside. Jerry reached under the seat and retrieved the red harness and leash he'd purchased for Gunter when the dog had first attached himself to him. Though Gunter had never actually used it, Jerry had kept it as a reminder of their early days together and the time he'd purchased a collar and leash for a dog that was invisible to most. Jerry smiled at the memory. He heard a woof and looked to see Gunter standing just inside the tent staring out at him. He gave the dog a nod and turned his attention back to Houdini. Holding up the harness, he realized it was too big for the lanky pup. He shoved it back under the seat and attached the leash to Houdini's collar. When he finished securing the pup, he roughed the dog's fur. "What are you doing here?"

Houdini answered with an eager kiss. Jerry responded with an affectionate scratch behind the ears. "No worries, I don't have time to dwell on the mysteries of the universe. You're here now, and there's nothing to be done about it, so we'd better get to work."

Gunter sounded a bark as if to say, *Hey, what about me?*

Jerry glanced at the dog, who now stood patiently waiting for Jerry to be done fiddling around with the pup. "I love you too, boy," Jerry said without speaking. "What say we do what we came here to do?"

Gunter smiled a K-9 smile and turned in eager circles. Houdini leapt from the Durango, pulling the leash behind him. Jerry shut the door and started to reach for the leash. Remembering the pup's previous antics, he knelt and called Houdini to him. This time, the puppy was eager to comply. As they walked toward the tent, Gunter turned and joined a group of women who sat near a table of refreshments. He nosed one of the women, who reached her left hand as if swatting a gnat. She straightened and brought up her right hand, which held a half-eaten doughnut. The woman caught him looking at her and shifted in her seat.

Gunter moved closer, sniffing the doughnut.

Great, Gunter has let his sweet tooth overrule his sense of duty.

As Jerry approached the tent, he saw Tisdale standing next to a park ranger who appeared to be in charge. Tisdale was peering over the man's shoulder at the clipboard he held in his hand.

Houdini sniffed the air and stretched as far as the leash would allow.

Jerry firmed his grip. "Houdini, heel. The pup hesitated and then returned to Jerry's side just as Jerry reached the park ranger.

The man lowered the clipboard and looked at Jerry with nary a smile. "How can I help you?"

"Actually, we are here to help you."

The park ranger blew out a sigh. "While we appreciate the public's desire to help, we have enough on our plates without having to worry about the locals getting lost. It's getting late, and it'll be dark before we know it. I can't risk anyone else going out there tonight."

Jerry stood his ground. "I'm not local. We are a team. I was passing through the area, heard the news, and thought I'd stop in to see if we can help."

The man looked down his nose at Houdini. "That pup's a bit young for this kind of work."

"I'm doing the work. The pup is in training." Jerry shrugged. "They have to start somewhere."

The park ranger raised an eyebrow. "You're a dog handler?"

Jerry resisted a laugh. *Not even close.* He decided to keep that to himself. "I usually work with a different dog."

"Yeah, well, maybe if your other dog were here, I'd consider it. As I said, we have an organized search that includes dogs more experienced in tracking. We've had our share of distractions today. I think maybe you two should get your training elsewhere. It's getting dark, and you're not familiar with the area."

Jerry firmed his chin.

Before he could respond, Tisdale appeared at his side. "Ask him if that distraction he's referring to is a beagle."

Jerry raised his hand and placed two fingers to his temple. "One of those distractions wouldn't happen to have been a beagle, would it?"

The park ranger lifted his chin. "What do you know about the beagle?"

Jerry waited for Tisdale to give him something. When he didn't, Jerry adlibbed, "I have the gift."

The man's jaw twitched. "Great, just what we

need, another psychic."

Jerry fought off a frown. Of course, there would have been others. The man's disappearance had been all over the news. Something like this was sure to bring out the best and the worst in people. While there were plenty of legit clairvoyants, there were also equally as many frauds, hoping to get lucky enough to get in a photo or say something that would get their name mentioned in the news. A thing like that went a long way to convince people of their legitimacy. Jerry pulled himself taller and pulled out his badge. "I am not just another psychic. I'm the Lead Paranormal Investigator for the Department of Defense."

The park ranger raised an eyebrow. "You're kidding, right?"

"If I were going to make up a lie, don't you think I'd come up with something better than that?" Jerry replied, pocketing the badge.

"You have a point." The man smiled for the first time since Jerry arrived and offered Jerry his hand. "Derek Monroe. Sorry about giving you a hard time. It's just that a search like this can be a quagmire."

Jerry understood the man's frustration. Conducting a search was bad enough, but doing so under the scrutiny of the media, where everything got reported in real time, was even worse. "Jerry McNeal. I'd like to have a look at your notes if you don't mind."

Derek rocked back on his heels. "I thought you said you were a psychic."

Tisdale snorted. "My thoughts exactly."

Ignoring Tisdale's remark, Jerry addressed his response to Derek. "I am. I can feel the man in question nearby, but I haven't homed in on him yet. I can waste time getting a feel for things or speed things up by finding out what you already know. This beagle seems to be an important piece of the puzzle. Why don't you start with that?"

Derek's jaw twitched. "You almost had me there for a few moments."

"What do you mean?"

"I mean, that beagle doesn't have a thing to do with the search." He turned and pointed up the path. "That blasted dog was running loose up there for god knows how long, sending our search dog on a wild goose chase."

The woman who'd been eating the donut pushed from her chair and hurried to where they were standing.

"What about the beagle?"

Derek waved the woman off. "It's okay, Miranda. This isn't the dog's owner."

"Then what does he want with it?"

Derek smiled at her. "Mr. McNeal, this is Miranda Knapp, one of our trusted volunteers. The beagle was running around much like that pup of yours, and she was the one who was finally able to catch the dog. She took him to the visitors' center when she went to get more ice."

Miranda bobbed her head. "I have a way with animals."

Houdini took this precise moment to break command and jump up, placing his paws on the woman's chest.

Miranda paled and took a step back.

"Houdini, down," Jerry said firmly.

Houdini lowered, but both he and Gunter stood watching the woman.

Something was off, but he couldn't put his finger on what that something was. Jerry stood his ground. "That beagle is a part of this, and I know it. I'd stake my reputation on it."

The color drained from Miranda's face as she looked Jerry up and down. "Who are you? Who is he?" she said to Derek before Jerry had a chance to answer.

"It's okay, Miranda. Mr. McNeal is just trying to help. As I said, the dog's not here. He was overheated, and Miranda left him at the welcome center so he could cool off. Do you want her to go get him?"

Jerry shook his head. "No, not right now."

One of the women who'd been standing at the refreshment table approached. "We need more ice. Miranda, do you want to go get some?"

"I bought all there was. There won't be any more

until tomorrow," Miranda barked. She turned, ignoring the woman as she focused on Jerry. "I'll go get the dog if you want, but I have to warn you, he doesn't seem to like men. I'll bring him, though, if you want."

Jerry looked at Tisdale, who shook his head. Jerry did the same. "No, I don't need to see him at the moment."

"But you might?"

"I'll let you know."

Miranda stormed off in the opposite direction, and the second woman followed. Jerry watched after them. "Mrs. Knapp a friend of yours?"

Derek chuckled. "Miranda's harmless. She's probably just afraid that you're interested in the dog. That thing about him not taking to men wasn't true. I think she threw that in there to warn you off. She plans to take him home if the owner isn't found."

Maybe... but something was off. That Gunter and Houdini had keyed on the woman told him there was more to her than met the eye. "That may be so, but the dog is a piece of the puzzle."

"You sound pretty sure of yourself."

"I am."

"Miranda is going to take him to the vet later to check for a microchip. If we can locate the owner, we might find a clue as to why the dog was out here in the first place."

Tisdale shook his head once more, and Jerry

instantly regretted having blocked him from getting into his head. He thought about opening communication but wasn't ready to have the man distracting him from the mission at hand. Jerry looked toward the path. "While I feel the dog to be connected to the case, I don't think the owner is going to give you anything."

"But you just said…"

"The dog is involved. The owner isn't." The man was close, Jerry could feel it, and he was injured. Of that, he was certain. He lowered his voice so no one would hear. "Listen, I'm going to go up the path a bit and see what I get."

Derek started to hand him a radio. "Take this in case you get turned around."

Jerry looked at Gunter and waved him off. "Save it for someone who needs it. I've got the dog."

Derek eyed the pup. "Up to you, but I wouldn't trust my life to a half-grown pup."

"We'll be fine."

"Suit yourself." Derek wrote something on the clipboard, and for a moment, Jerry thought the man was going to ask him to sign a release. Instead, he reached into an envelope and pulled out a strip of fabric. "This is from the shirt the man wore the day before he went missing. Let the pup get a whiff, but keep him on a leash."

Jerry knelt and was pleased to see both the pup and Gunter sniff the remnant. "Good, now find."

Houdini yipped and sniffed the air, obviously ready to get to work. Gunter, on the other hand, lowered his nose to the ground, sniffing his way to the refreshment table. Miranda sat behind the table, talking with several others. She saw him watching and offered a smile. Too much of one to be labeled genuine. He'd been watching her since his arrival into the tent and had yet to see her with such a toothy grin. *What's your deal, lady? Easy, McNeal, don't go reading anything into it. She's probably just trying to win you over so you don't try and lay claim to the dog.* Houdini pulled at the leash, ambling off in the opposite direction. *Don't worry, lady, I assure you I have my hands full with the ones I have.* Jerry turned, following the pup's lead.

They'd no sooner left the enclosure when Houdini started toward the parking lot.

"Don't let the pup lead you astray, McNeal. The search area is up that path," Derek called after him.

The path in question was a dirt path with railroad timbers spaced evenly the length of it to act as stairs. Each looked to have been there for some time as most were sunk in the well-worn path that led the way up the mountain. "Says who?"

"Says the five other dogs and their handlers that went before him."

Jerry tugged on the pup's leash. "Houdini, heel." Houdini hesitated, then fell into step beside him. While Jerry was happy the pup listened, he wasn't pleased he'd ordered the pup to comply. If Max had, in fact, been working with the dog, the animal would have some sense of what was expected of him. Houdini wasn't like other dogs – his dad was a ghost. Maybe that heritage meant nothing, or perhaps it meant he knew things others did not. Even Gunter had refused to follow them up the path, and he understood the mission at hand. Jerry stilled, balled the sliver of shirt in his hand, and concentrated on the feeling.

We're going the wrong way.

He'd no sooner had the thought than his cell phone chimed. Jerry pulled it from his pocket and saw a text from April. > *This is Max again. You're cold.*

Jerry sighed. Even Max knew he was heading the wrong way, and she wasn't even there. His cell chimed again. Jerry read the message from Max.> *Not you, him. He's cold.*

Jerry typed his reply. >*Yes, I'm having him turn around.*

Max> *I don't understand.*

Jerry sighed. *I hope the man's condition isn't as serious as it feels. We've already wasted valuable time.* Jerry > *I know we're on the wrong trail. I'm having Houdini turn around.*

Max> *Not Houdini, the man. The man is cold. Tell Houdini to find him. Granny said that's why he is there. To help find the man. She said you need to trust him.*

Jerry dropped to a crouch and let the pup smell the cloth once more. "Houdini, find."

The pup pressed his nose to the fabric, wagging his tail. When finished, he started back the way they'd just come, hesitating once more when he reached the end of his lead. Jerry started after him, and the pup continued to pull him forward until he slipped right out of the collar. Jerry stood there with leash and collar in hand, watching Houdini race down the hill.

Jerry addressed the sky. "You want me to trust him, I will. But if he gets hurt, it's on you."
From a distance, Derek's voice sang out. "McNeal, you'd better be hurt or dead. It's the only excuse I'll accept for allowing that dog to run free!"

Chapter Seven

As Jerry started down the path, an image of a giant pink rabbit came to mind. A second later, the woman with the pink hair appeared, blocking his path. Jerry held up his hand. "Not now."

She blinked. "But…"

"No buts. Whatever it is can wait. I've got to find my dog."

The spirit pointed down the slope. "That's what I came to tell you. He's right down there."

"I know which way he went," Jerry said, stepping around her. He also knew that Houdini wasn't like other dogs, and he needed to find him before he did anything to raise suspicion. The last thing he needed was for someone to see the pup disappear.

Derek met him at the base of the path, his face so red, he looked as if he was about to explode. He waited for Jerry to get close and held his hand sideways above his head. "McNeal, I've had it up to here with you and that dog. I gave you a chance to join in the search, and you threw it in my face by letting that pup run amuck. Don't you give me any bull about letting him find his way. He's running through the place, destroying the scent. It's a search area, not a doggie playground."

Jerry understood the man's frustration; however, unfortunately for Derek, the man had caught him at a bad time. From the moment he entered the park, he'd encountered nothing but delays. How was he supposed to find the coach when his psychic energy was being blocked at every turn? Jerry worked to keep his voice even. "My dog is following a lead."

Derek laughed, but the humor didn't reach his eyes. "I'm asking you politely to leave and take the shepherd with you."

"Sure. After we conclude our search." Jerry started to move past, and Derek caught him by the arm.

Instantly, Gunter appeared at Jerry's side, teeth bared.

Jerry jerked his arm free and gave a subtle hand command to settle the dog. "I know you're just doing your job, but I would advise you to keep your hands to yourself."

Derek jerked his thumb toward the parking lot. "And I would advise you to leave the property before I have you arrested. I'm done playing nice because you have a badge. You can go on your own, or I'll make a call and have you escorted out the gate."

Gunter kept a watchful eye as Jerry rocked back on his heels. "This is government property, yes?"

Derek narrowed his eyes. "You know it is."

"The way I see it, since I work for the government, this is technically my office." Jerry knew he was being a jerk, but the guy was getting on his nerves.

"Your office! I'm the park ranger, and I'm pretty sure I outrank you."

Not likely. Jerry held his tongue as Derek continued his tirade.

"You'll be lucky to have a job when I'm through with you."

Jerry sighed in resignation. If he was going to get anything accomplished, he was going to have to bring out the big guns. He reached into his front pocket and fished out his wallet. Opening it, he retrieved one of Fred's business cards, handing it to the guy.

Derek studied the card. "What's this?"

My get-out-of-jail-free card. Jerry shrugged. "You want to have me fired, that there is the number to my boss. Now, if you'll excuse me, I'm going to go do my thing."

"W-what thing is that?" That Derek was

stuttering showed just how angry he was.

"I'm going to find your guy so I can be on my way." Jerry turned. Gunter took off in front of him, leading him in the opposite direction of where he'd parked.

"I told you the search was up that hill!" Derek bellowed after him.

"Yes, but my dog tells me our guy is this way."

Derek caught up with him just as Jerry reached the tent. "McNeal, you're either extremely cocky or incredibly naive. You're telling me you're going to place your fate in a pup that hasn't listened to a single command since you arrived?"

Gunter looked to make sure he was following before skirting around the tent.

Jerry followed. "Yep."

"If you're wrong, I'm making the call," Derek warned.

"You can make it now, for all I care," Jerry replied. Not that it mattered, as he was certain they were close to finding what they'd been looking for. Not only were his spidey senses screaming, but Houdini and the whole ghostly entourage were now focused on a bright red pickup truck parked a short distance away. While Gunter had turned to look at him, Houdini was licking the gravel beneath the bed of the truck. The spirit with the pink hair stood next to Tisdale, who casually leaned against the back bumper of the truck. A hard shell covered the truck bed. Jerry tested it, not surprised to find it locked.

Derek stepped up beside him. "What do you want with Miranda's truck?"

Miranda, of course. Gunter wasn't interested in the donuts. He knew the woman to be involved. Good boy, Gunter. Sorry I doubted you again. Jerry looked at the tent. "Call Mrs. Knapp over. I want to look inside the truck."

Derek hesitated. "I've known Miranda a long time. You can't possibly think she's involved with this."

Jerry held his ground. "Get her here and tell her to bring her keys. While you're at it, have them send Med Flight to this location."

Derek's face paled. "Med Flight?"

Jerry pointed to Houdini. "My dog thinks I should have a look inside, and my feeling is the man isn't dead."

"That pup isn't interested in the truck," Derek scoffed. "He's keyed on something underneath."

Following Gunter's lead, Houdini took that particular time to sit back on his haunches, barking at the truck.

Jerry jumped on the back bumper and tried to pry open the cover. "Make the call! And find those keys!"

Derek keyed his radio. "Miranda Knapp, return to your vehicle immediately."

Tisdale stuck his head through the bed of the

truck and pulled it out once more. He frowned at Jerry. "Better hurry things up there, boss."

Jerry glared at Derek. "Get Med Flight here now!"

Derek pushed back. "You're barking commands on a hunch. You don't know if the guy's even in there, much less what his condition is. The ambulance is stationed at the welcome center. I'll get them started, and they can make the call."

Jerry jumped to the dirt, took out his cell, and called Fred. "Send Med Flight to my location."

"Done!" Fred's voice boomed through the phone.

That was what he liked about Fred's actions before reactions.

"I take it you found the guy."

"Nope, the dogs did," Jerry replied.

"Dogs?"

"The search dogs," Jerry said, covering his mistake and ending the call before Fred could respond. Seeing a text from Max, he swiped to open it.

Max> *Ask the donut lady about the dog.* That Max had picked up on any of this didn't surprise him. Jerry smiled and pocketed his phone.

"Who was that?" Derek asked.

Jerry blew out a sigh. "We don't have time to play twenty questions. Find me a crowbar. If we don't get the guy out of there, we will need a meat wagon instead of a helicopter."

Gunter growled, and once again, Houdini followed his father's lead.

Jerry looked to see Miranda Knapp hurrying across the parking lot.

"GET AWAY FROM MY TRUCK!" she yelled as she neared.

Derek patted the air with his hands. "Take it easy, Miranda. I'm sure this is all a mistake. His dog took an interest in your truck, and we just have to take a look inside."

"Not without a warrant," she said between breaths. "I watch *CSI*. I know my rights."

She started toward the driver's side door, stopping when Houdini moved between her and the truck, emitting a low growl. To Derek and Miranda, the pup appeared to be acting on its own accord, but Jerry knew him only to be imitating Gunter, who stood beside him doing the same.

Jerry squared his shoulders. "Then you know homicide carries a heftier sentence than bodily harm. If you don't open the shell, that man will die."

"What man? I...I don't know what you're talking about. I just came to show my support."

"That's not why you're here, and you know it." Jerry's words were calm and deliberate.

"Okay, you got me. I came to bring donuts and ice," Miranda sneered.

"More ice than anyone would need, which is why

the truck is still sweating," Jerry replied. "But you messed up. You bought the ice because you thought you killed him. You thought it would buy you some time and help to diffuse the smell, but I have news for you. The coach is not dead."

Miranda's eyes darted to the truck bed.

Jerry took a step closer. "That's right. You can still make this right, Miranda. Coach is hurt badly and needs our help. Give me the keys so we can get him out of there."

Miranda didn't move.

Jerry thought about tackling the woman, but could hear the ambulance in the distance and knew help was only a couple moments away. "Give me the keys, Miranda." An image of Miranda releasing the dog came to mind. Jerry looked at Derek. "She brought the dog."

Miranda's brows knitted. "I don't know what you're talking about. I don't own a dog."

"The beagle."

"Oh, him. He's not mine. I just drove him to the visitors' center." She shrugged a hapless shrug. "Unless no one claims him. Then he'll be mine."

Jerry firmed his stance and looked her in the eye. "You brought him here."

"No, I did not." Miranda pointed to Derek. "Ask him, he'll tell you."

"We arrived at the same time, and there wasn't a dog," Derek said, confirming her story.

Jerry wasn't buying it. Not only did he feel it, but Max wouldn't have keyed on the dog if it wasn't connected. "She brought the beagle. I know it as well as I know my own name."

"The search team found the beagle hours after we arrived and brought him to camp. By the time they brought the poor guy down the mountain path, the dog had nearly run himself to death."

Jerry directed his comment to Miranda. "Then you brought him before the search and set him loose before you made the call to let the search teams know where to look."

Miranda gasped, then covered with a cough.

Jerry pulled himself taller. "You want to know how I know, don't you?

Miranda's gaze darted from side to side as if she were considering making a break for it. Jerry looked at Gunter and Houdini, both of whom were watching the woman as if daring her to run. Jerry softened his tone to gain her trust. "I'm a psychic, Miranda. It's my job to know those things. My gift led me here. It's also how I know the coach isn't dead. I can feel him. You watch *CSI*. You know they will go easier on you if you cooperate. Now give me the keys so we can get him out of there."

Miranda held out her hand, dropping the keys into his. As he wrapped his fingers around them, the feeling of impending doom lifted. He tossed the keys to Derek. "Check the back."

Miranda started forward, and Gunter and Houdini moved in front of her, stopping her in her tracks.

"He's here!" Derek called from the rear of the truck. "He's alive, but I don't know for how long." The ambulance slowed near the tent. Derek whistled a shrill whistle to get their attention. "HEY!"

Houdini turned toward the siren and emitted an eager yip. Gunter gave a sharp woof, and Houdini focused on Miranda once more. If not for the seriousness of the current situation, Jerry would have taken a moment to fully appreciate the fact that Gunter was helping train the pup.

The ambulance pulled to where they were standing, and two men piled out. One stopped at the back to gather equipment while the other hurried to where Derek now stood inside the truck bed. Derek moved aside, then finally relinquished his place altogether when the second man neared pulling a gurney. The EMT left the gurney and climbed into the bed of the truck with his partner.

Derek keyed the radio. "Command to all search teams. We've found the coach. I repeat, we've found the coach. All teams return to base." Derek sighed. "I'm not a doctor, but it looks pretty bad. The paramedic said he's lucky to be alive."

Hearing the news, tears spilled out of Miranda's eyes. "You mean you were right? I didn't kill him?"

Derek stiffened. "You're saying you did that to

him?"

Jerry resisted rolling his eyes and struggled to keep from reminding the park ranger that the victim was in Miranda's truck but decided against it, thinking that perhaps the guy was in shock from what he'd just seen.

Miranda wrung her hands together. "I thought I'd killed him. I hadn't meant to. It just kind of happened. He's going to live, right?"

Derek looked toward the truck bed. "I don't know, Miranda. He's pretty messed up. What'd you hit him with? A shovel?"

Miranda's face puckered. "A shovel? No, of course not. I used a baseball bat. Pretty fitting if you ask me. That man's been harping on my swing since I was a kid. He might not have thought I remembered, but I do, and it burns me to no end. Now he's doing the same thing to my daughter. Day after day, I watched her spirit dwindle as he sat her out game after game. I know what it's like to sit on the bench while all your friends get to play. And I'm telling you, it's not fair. Leah is a darn good player. She's only in a batting slump because the guy's a terrible coach." A sly smile touched her lips. "I guess I fixed that. He won't be coaching anytime soon. I didn't mean to hit him. I just wanted to talk to him. Then he said something about the apple not falling far from the tree, and I guess I just snapped. I guess I got a bit carried away. I'm glad he's alive. I'm also glad Leah will be getting a new coach. Word will get out, and whoever it is will know I'm serious when I tell them they'd better not make my daughter sit out the game. I can't wait to tell Leah when I get home. She'll be thrilled she gets to play."

Jerry cocked an eyebrow at Derek. "Do you want to tell her, or should I?"

Derek took the lead. "Miranda, I hate to be the bearer of bad news, but you're not going home."

"Sure I am. You said he's alive."

"He is, but not by much. You nearly killed him."

"It wasn't like it was premeditated or anything." She jabbed a thumb in Jerry's direction. "You heard him. I cooperated, so they'll go easy on me."

Derek remained stone-faced. "According to the paramedic, the only reason Coach hasn't bled to death is because you have him packed in so much ice, it slowed the bleeding."

"You know it was a pain in the tush filling that bed with all that ice. I had to go to seven different stores. Now I see it was worth it because I saved his life." Miranda smiled a triumphant smile. "You know, this feels pretty darn good. I've never been a hero before. Wait until word gets out. Won't I be the talk of town?"

Derek opened his mouth, and Jerry waved him off. The last thing he wanted was for the woman to shut down before anyone could get an official confession from her.

Chapter Eight

Houdini and Gunter lay in the grass with the sun beating down on them as Jerry leaned against the Durango. He'd already given the cop his rendition of the events and stood watching as the helicopter carrying the coach spooled up. Though no one shared Miranda's belief she was a hero, her actions had proven to be the only reason the man was still alive. Even after the police arrived to take her to the station, the woman remained adamant she'd done what she did to protect her daughter.

As the helo lifted off, Jerry's mind drifted to Max and April and how quickly April had sped into the parking lot when Max had texted her saying she needed help. April had suffered at the hands of her husband, only taking steps when the abuse threatened to spill out onto her daughter. He closed his eyes, thinking about the two and how they meant more to him than anything else. He knew without question that he, too, would go to great lengths to see them both safe. While he didn't condone Miranda's course of action, he understood where her motivation came from.

The thought no sooner came to him than his cell phone rang, alerting him to Max's call. He swiped to answer. "I was just thinking about you."

"You were?"

"Yep. I was getting ready to call and let you know we found the coach."

Max giggled. "I already know that."

"You felt it?"

"No, I saw it on the news. I watched them load the coach onto the helicopter. It just lifted off. I looked for you, but I didn't see you. I knew you were there, though, because I felt it. They said he is in critical condition, but I know he's going to make it because I can feel that too."

"Yeah, Max, I can feel it too."

"I've been thinking."

Jerry smiled. "About what?"

"I think I sent Houdini to you."

"How so?"

"I was watching the videos and worried they wouldn't find the coach in time. Then I started thinking about how I've been working with Houdini, and he's really good at finding things. I mean really good. I hide things and don't even tell him. I just think about what it is and where I hid it, and he finds them and brings them to me. I figure it is because he's part ghost, and that makes him special. I started thinking that if he was there with you, he would be able to help you find Coach."

As crazy as it sounded, it was the only thing that made sense. "So you're saying you concentrated on him coming to me, and he disappeared?"

"Sort of. I thought about it a lot. But I didn't see him disappear. He was just walking around the yard, sniffing everything. I mean, I thought about it, but I didn't really think it would actually work. And when he kept sniffing the yard, I kind of forgot about it. I was talking to Chloe when my phone died. I ran in to plug it in, and when I came back out, I saw he was missing and thought he'd run away. That's when me and Mom went looking for him."

Jerry considered her words. "Max, let's try a little experiment. I'm going to try and send Houdini to you, and I want you to think about him and will him to come to you."

"Okay. But I'm not sure it will work."

Jerry frowned. "Why not?"

"Because when we thought he was missing, both me and Mom were thinking about him. We called and called, and he didn't come."

She has a point. "Let's give it a try anyway. Maybe since he's here and you are there, it will work."

"Do you want me to do it now?" Max asked.

"Yes. I'll count to three, and we'll both do it. One. Two. Three." Jerry stared at Houdini. *Go see Max. Go to Max. Max needs you.* As he willed the dog to go, Max called to him. After several unsuccessful moments, Jerry sighed. "I guess it's not going to work this time."

Max giggled.

Jerry looked to where Houdini had just been lying beside his ghostly dad. "He's gone."

Max giggled once more. "That's because he's here."

Jerry could hardly believe his ears. "Is he okay? How's he acting?"

"He's great. He's getting a drink."

Jerry wanted to ask if the dog was in one piece, but since Max wasn't hysterically screaming that the water Houdini was drinking was running through him, that was a good sign. "That is amazing." Jerry heard a squeaky yawn and looked to see Gunter staring at him as if to say, *What's the big deal? I do it all the time.* Jerry laughed.

"What's so funny?"

"I was laughing at Gunter. He doesn't find Houdini's disappearing as exciting as we do. Is your mom close?"

"No, she's inside fixing dinner."

"Okay, I won't bother her. Just tell her I'm heading out and to give me a call when she has a free moment."

"Okay, Jerry, see ya."

Jerry had no sooner ended the call than his cell phone rang, displaying the words "anonymous call." As he swiped to answer, the hair on the back of his neck stood on end.

"I hear tell you're on your way to Texas."

Jerry opened the door to the Durango, placed the phone on speaker, slid into the seat, and pushed the overhead button that granted him quick access to Fred. "Fabel. How can I help you?"

"Jerry, my friend, call me Mario. After all, we're practically family."

Jerry kept his voice even. "Last I checked, your name wasn't listed on my family tree."

"Semantics, my friend. I still owe you for finding my sister and helping her spirit find peace."

Jerry leaned his head against the driver's seat and blew out a sigh. "What can I do for you, Fabel?"

"Again with the last name."

"I'm a Marine. It's what we do."

"Okay, I'll let it slide."

"That's big of you. Now, what can I help you with?"

"Actually, I called to give you a bit of brotherly advice. Since we're family and all."

Jerry had plenty of men who, even though they weren't listed on the family tree, he readily accepted as brothers. Mario Fabel wasn't one of them. Still, that the man had picked up the phone to call intrigued him. "I'm listening."

"Word on the street is you're traveling to Texas because of one Antonio Maioriello, who may or may not still be among the living. Now, I'm not worried about Antonio. That man's not worth the paper his birth certificate is printed on. Bruno Deluca, the fellow he snitched on, now he's another story. When my godfather told me stories of the boogeyman, those stories were about Bruno Deluca."

Fred had said Deluca was bad news, which meant Mario was taking a chance warning him off. Mario Fabel wasn't a lightweight, and for him to be afraid of the guy said a lot. An image of the bodach from the movie *Odd Thomas* came to mind. Black and scary, the creature in the movie was a dark entity. A shiver raced through him. Gunter appeared in the seat beside him. Jerry shook off the image as he ran his fingers through the dog's fur.

Jerry's phone buzzed. He looked and saw a message from Fred.

Fred> *Your going to Texas is not public knowledge.*

Jerry spoke into the phone. "I wasn't aware anyone knew I was going to Texas. Are you saying we have a leak?"

"Not that I'm aware of. I only heard that Deluca is making noise, and someone promised to send someone to look into the situation. Word on the street is Antonio Maioriello is dead, so, as you may suspect, my source found this highly amusing and made cracks about them sending the Ghostbusters. I, on the other hand, figured they would send someone even better – that someone being you. Some may scoff, but you made me a believer." Mario chuckled. "Now that I think about it, I guess I shouldn't have worried about you. A man that can do what you do probably already knows what's in store for him on the other end."

I don't have a clue. He decided to keep his vulnerabilities to himself. "I appreciate the heads-up, Mario."

The chuckle turned into a full laugh. "You used my first name. Does that mean you believe me?"

"I do."

"Good. I'll keep my ear to the ground and let you know if I hear anything. You think of anything else, say the word. I don't mind shaking a few trees to see what falls loose."

"Don't do anything that'll put a target on your back," Jerry warned.

Mario sniffed. "Aw geez, don't that beat all. You're worried about me."

Jerry smiled. "You said it yourself, we're family."

"You're an all right dude, Jerry McNeal. In another life, I believe we could have been good friends."

"In another life," Jerry agreed. Before he could say anything else, Mario ended the call. Jerry looked at the dash. "Did you get everything?"

Fred's voice boomed inside the cab of the SUV. "You two sounded pretty chummy."

"What's that saying? Keep your friends close and your enemies closer."

"The question is do you consider Mario your friend or your enemy?"

Jerry laughed. "Depends on what day it is. Do you think he was telling the truth about how he knew I was heading to Texas?"

"We keep your whereabouts close to home. Just to be sure, I'll shake some trees of my own. What about your current situation?"

"I may have ruffled some feathers playing king of the roost, but we found our guy. He's headed to the hospital as we speak."

"I take it that means you're heading out."

Jerry pushed the start button on the dash. "Yep."

"What are you going to do with the pup?"

Nothing now. "Who told you?"

"You did, when you said 'dogs.' Anyone else and I wouldn't have thought anything of it. But you aren't known to slip up like that. I didn't realize you'd taken him with you."

Fib, Jerry, it will be easier. The trouble with that was twofold. Jerry wasn't a good liar and Fred's BS detector was never wrong. "I didn't."

"I'm not following you."

Jerry glanced at Gunter. "Yes, you are."

"Meaning?"

"Meaning that possibility that's rolling around in your head right now is precisely what happened."

"You're saying that pup just showed up?"

"Yep."

"Just appeared out of nowhere?"

"Yep. And left the same way he came when all was said and done."

"How is that even possible?"

Jerry thought about Max's theory. "You're the brainiac, you tell me. One minute, I'm sitting there trying to worm my way past the gate guard, and the next, she's letting me through the gate because she thinks I'm part of the search team. I look in the mirror to see Gunter. I figured he'd allowed the woman to see him to get me through the gate. By the time we get to the command center, Houdini is there too. That he wasn't wearing a collar or leash nearly got us both kicked out of the park."

Fred chuckled. "You sure it wasn't because of your attitude?"

That Fred had already been read in on the situation didn't surprise him. It didn't matter how far-reaching the problem. Fred was a man that got answers to all his questions, even those he had yet to ask. "You heard about that, did you?"

"Let's just say after you gave your account of the

woman's confession, I received a call saying your methods were a bit unconventional and to further ask if your statement was credible."

"What'd you tell them?"

"You're not wearing handcuffs, are you? You know, it would be a lot easier if you lead with your badge instead of waiting until you make them angry enough to threaten to kick you out of a place."

"I thought maybe I could regale them with my good looks and charm."

Fred laughed a hearty laugh.

"It wasn't that funny," Jerry said dryly.

"Funny, no. Frustrating, yes."

"How so?"

"Because you still haven't gotten comfortable with the badge."

Jerry squirmed in his seat and was grateful Fred couldn't see through the dash. "You seem to have forgotten I used to be a state police officer."

"That's not the badge I'm talking about."

Fred was right, and Jerry knew it. "It took most of my life to wrap my head around this gift of mine. I think it's fair to ask for a bit more time before expecting me to whip out the badge you gave me and proclaim I'm a ghostbuster."

"You mean the lead paranormal investigator for the Department of Defense."

Jerry looked at the dash. "Let me ask you this. Say you're Johnny Nobody who lives in a cabin in the woods in the heart of the country. I show up on your porch, flash you my badge, and rattle off my title. Are you going to think, *Cool, a psychic* or *Look, it's a freaking ghostbuster?*"

Fred laughed.

"Stop laughing. I'm being serious."

"That wasn't me laughing. It was Barney."

"I'm taking it he went with ghostbuster?"

"No, he went with a shovel."

"Come again?"

Barney's voice floated through the speakers. "You show up at a random cabin in the woods unannounced, and you've probably found yourself someone who's going to shoot first and ask questions later. People have long been afraid of the government. Throw in the internet and what people watch on the news, and the fear is worse than ever before. If you're going to go walking in the woods, I wouldn't advise flashing any badges unless you're waving a white flag and someone knows you're coming. Even then, you can't be sure you're not going to catch some lead in your behind."

It wasn't the first time Barney had floated a conspiracy theory. Jerry smiled at the dash. "Barney, why is it I get the feeling you've got yourself a little cabin in the woods?"

"Who said my cabin is small?" Barney's words held no hint of humor.

Jerry smiled. Obviously, there was more to the

man than met the eye.

Fred cut in. "You were right about the dog. Turns out Mrs. Knapp drove to a shelter two towns over and rescued that dog for the precise reason of throwing the search team off their tracks. It was she who supposedly went to the man's house and got the shirt the dogs were using to search the trail. Only she didn't use the shirt the wife gave her. She used the one she'd taken off of him when she beaned him. It was the same shirt she'd ripped a piece off and tied to the beagle, knowing he would leave enough scent in the search area to send the dogs on a wild goose chase. What she didn't count on was you keying on the dog. She's sticking by her story of being upset that the coach told her she had a lousy swing. The joke's on him, don't you think?"

"How's that?"

Fred laughed. "Seems her swing's improved over the years."

Gunter gave a squeaky yawn and looked at him as if to say, *Your boss is a funny guy.*

Jerry smiled and reached over to scratch the canine behind the ear. "Humor him. He has his moments."

Chapter Nine

Jerry looked in the rearview mirror as he was exiting the park and saw Tisdale looking back at him. He glanced at Gunter, who was leaning against the back of the front passenger seat. Even though the front seat was Gunter's rightful spot, it seemed odd to see the lawman sitting in the back. Especially since the man had already made such a big deal about not wishing to sit there. Jerry checked the road in front and looked in the rearview mirror once more.

Tisdale pushed back his hat to meet Jerry's gaze. "You look like you've seen a ghost. What's troubling you, son?"

Jerry smiled an easy smile. "I've seen more than a few spirits in my time, but some surprise me more than others. This morning, you were ready to fight for this seat. Now you're sitting back there like a judge being chauffeured to a trial."

"I figured the dog earned that spot today."

"Houdini helped too," Jerry reminded him.

"Houdini? That be the pup's name?"

Jerry nodded. "Yep."

"He did good. You know he's not like other dogs, don't you?"

Jerry chuckled. "You mean the whole disappearing and reappearing thing? Yes, I know."

"Then you also know he's going to be a force to be reckoned with one day. Especially with that one there showing him the ropes."

Jerry slid a quick glance to Gunter. "We all need our mentors."

"Even you?" Tisdale asked.

Jerry nodded once more. "I've had a couple. If I had to choose, I would say my grandmother and my old boss had the most influence on me." Instantly, Seltzer came to mind. Jerry made a mental note to call him.

"I believe it's safe to assume your grandmother knew about this gift of yours. What about your boss?"

Jerry smiled. "I guess Seltzer knows just about everything there is to know about me."

"And yet you're not still working for him."

Traffic slowed. Jerry glanced in the side mirror and moved to the left lane to pass. "That's right."

"Why not?" Tisdale pressed.

Jerry shrugged. "It's a long story."

"It's a long way to Texas. You got anything better to talk about?"

Jerry laughed a half laugh as he checked the mirror and maneuvered back to the right lane. "No, I don't suppose I do."

"You were an officer of the law, yes?"

Jerry searched his mind. He didn't recall ever telling Tisdale he was a state trooper. *But I did mention it when speaking with Fred a few moments ago. How does he keep getting in my mind?* He blocked Tisdale from getting answers he didn't want him to have. "I was a trooper with the Pennsylvania State Police Department."

"Trooper?"

Jerry decided to keep his answer simple. "State police have jurisdiction within the state they are working in."

"You wore a star?"

"A badge," Jerry corrected.

"You left that job for the one you have now?"

Jerry shook his head. "No, I got this one after I left."

"You didn't like the trooper job?"

Jerry was starting to regret agreeing to answer Tisdale's questions. "It's a little more complicated than that."

"You had a job. You left the job. I don't see the complication."

"Why does this suddenly feel like an inquisition?"

"I'm not trying to rattle your cage. I'm just trying to figure out what kind of man you are. Your tactics need some finessing, but you were able to get the job done there today. This trooper job, why'd you quit?"

"They wanted me to follow the rules." As lame as it sounded, it was the truth.

"Meaning they wanted you to do the job they hired you for."

"That about sums it up."

"I noticed that about you. You don't like to play by the rules. Can't say as I blame you. I never liked being told what to do. It alienated me from people I worked with."

Jerry looked in the mirror as if seeing the man for the first time. "You're saying you were the lone ranger?"

"I worked alone, yes." The lack of humor in Tisdale's remark showed he didn't get the joke.

Jerry bit his lip to keep from laughing, not wishing to explain why he found the comment so amusing.

Gunter groaned.

Jerry glanced at the dog. "What? It was funny."

Gunter disappeared.

Tisdale appeared in the front seat. "Did I miss something?"

Jerry sighed. "Apparently not."

"You said your boss knew about you. Was that always the case?" Tisdale asked, picking up where he'd left off.

Jerry shook his head. "No. Not at first."

"Because you didn't want to tell him, or you didn't want him to know?"

Jerry thought about that for a moment. "A bit of both, I suppose. I wasn't comfortable with my gift at the time."

Tisdale cut him off. "If you don't like it, why do you call it a gift?"

"It's what my grandmother called it," Jerry replied.

"But you didn't believe her?"

"Not at the time. It's not easy being different. Kids can be cruel. Even the ones who are supposed to be your friends end up wanting something from you."

"But you do now?"

"I do."

"What changed?"

Jerry skirted around a slow-moving car, then returned to the right lane. "I'm not really sure. I guess it is just having people who believe in me and what I do."

"Your grandmother believed in you and knew what you could do, so why didn't you believe her?"

Because I was a jerk. Jerry kept that thought to himself. "Because your grandmother is supposed to believe in you even if they don't."

Tisdale scoffed. "Maybe in your world. My grandmother told me I was a lying, thieving varmint that would never amount to anything."

Jerry smiled. "I'd love to hear the story behind that."

"You're changing the subject," Tisdale said tersely.

"There are a lot of things about my life I would change if I had the chance. I've made my peace with my family and don't care to go into the details."

Tisdale sighed. "Fair enough. This Seltzer guy, you said he knows about the gift. What did you say to convince him?"

"I didn't say anything – not at first, anyway. I had just gotten out of the Marines and had a buddy who had joined the force. He seemed to like it well enough, so I applied."

"Then it was the buddy who smoothed the road for you."

"No, he was with the state police in Arizona. I'd just returned from the desert and wasn't interested in moving anywhere hot. I did some checking and ended up applying for a post in Pennsylvania. Best move I ever made in so many ways."

"How's that?"

"The state is among the prettiest places I've ever seen. The rolling hills, snow globe towns, the people. Seltzer and his wife, June, practically adopted me."

"People don't like adopting boys, much less grown men." Tisdale's voice held an edge Jerry hadn't heard from him before.

"I didn't say they adopted me. I said they practically adopted me. It was a figure of speech, meaning they took me under their wing and kind of looked out for me."

"Then you were lucky."

"I was," Jerry agreed.

"Was it because of that gift of yours?"

"No, the sergeant and his wife are just those kind of people."

"What kind of people is that?"

"People with big hearts who give more than they take. They took in a pregnant woman some months back. It's just what they do."

"Do-gooders. In my experience, they always have an agenda."

Jerry glanced at Tisdale, waiting for him to say more. When he didn't, Jerry picked up his story. "I started out with a unit in Philly – Philadelphia," Jerry clarified. "When my rotation was up, I requested a unit in Chambersburg – I've never done well with my gift in large cities and the smaller town seemed like a good fit. Seltzer and his wife welcomed me from day one of my arrival at the station. I'd been on the job in Chambersburg a couple of weeks, and while I'd gotten plenty of psychic hits, this one was a doozy. I knew there was going to be trouble, and I knew it was going to be bad. I was supposed to be going to Carlisle that day, and the moment I started out in that direction, I knew I was heading the wrong way. I tried to shake it off, but the wave just kept coming at me until I had to call and get someone to relieve me. When I got back to the station, Seltzer called me into his office and told me if I was sick to go home. I told him I wasn't sick and took a chance by telling him the truth."

"He believed you?"

"He said he did, but I knew he didn't."

"Did that bother you?"

"No, I was used to people not believing me." Jerry gripped the wheel, remembering his time with the Marines. "The thing is, even though he didn't believe me, he was willing to give me the benefit of the doubt. He told me to follow my spidey senses and see where they led."

"Spidey senses?"

Jerry started to tell him about Spider-Man but knew that would derail the conversation. "It's what Seltzer calls my gift."

"And that's it. He just let you go off chasing things he didn't understand?"

Jerry chuckled. "In a nutshell, yes. But I think he would have been happier if it actually worked that way."

"I'm not following you."

"The way this thing works is I know something's going to happen, but I don't always know what or when. So, while I knew something bad was going to happen, that's all I knew."

"In other words, instead of working, you were now sitting around twiddling your thumbs."

"Correct. I worked a few small cases, but I stayed in the area waiting for it. The feeling kept building and building. Then one of our troopers called in an officer in pursuit of a subject involved in a fatal shooting. Seltzer was thrilled, thinking this was the big thing I'd told him about, but I knew this wasn't what we needed to be worried about. It was near shift change, so there were plenty of troopers on site. Everyone filed out of the station, Seltzer included. When he filed past me, I knew it was him that my gift had pegged on."

"Did you tell him?"

"No, he wouldn't have believed me. I knew it as sure as I knew him to be my target. So, I hung back, following him. The chase was one that cops both pray for and hope they are never a part of, reaching speeds well over a hundred miles an hour. I'm following behind the sergeant, and we're going faster and faster, and I'll be honest, I was pretty close to backing off when Seltzer slowed and started cruising. While I was relieved, my radar was still humming like mad. Once he started cruising, he just kept on slowing until he finally rolled to a stop in the gravel at the bottom of the hill. I knew something was wrong but didn't know what, so I didn't phone it in. When I got to his cruiser, he was just sitting there covered in sweat. I knocked on the window, but he didn't respond. He wasn't aware of me or the spirit sitting next to him."

Tisdale jerked his head around. "Spirit?"

"I don't know who it was because he never spoke. He could understand me, though, as I got him to unlock Seltzer's door so I didn't have to break the window."

"What was wrong with him?"

"Some kind of panic attack or something. He didn't talk for nearly twenty minutes. Later, he told me he was listening to the radio and was so caught up in the chase that he didn't realize how fast he was going. Said he looked down, saw he was pegged at over a hundred and thirty, and knew there'd be nothing left of him if he crashed. He said an image of his wife flashed in his mind. He said he wasn't scared of dying, but the thought of leaving June a widow made his heart clench. He took his foot off the gas and just let it coast. If anyone else had been there that day, they would have called it in, and he'd have been hauled off in an ambulance. Something like that could have impacted the man's career. As it was, I let the air out of his tire, and we passed the incident off as him having a flat."

Tisdale was quiet for a moment. "How fast are

we going now?"

Jerry checked the speedometer. Eighty. He surveyed his surroundings, then pressed the gas, the hemi engine reaching a hundred in seconds. "We were going a lot faster than this," he said, easing off the gas.

"I can see where that might invigorate a man," Tisdale replied. "I can also see why the man is beholden to you."

"It's not something I've ever held over his head." Actually, neither of them had ever mentioned it again.

"You wouldn't have to. A man does something like that for me, and I would know I could count on him when the chips were down. You're a decent man, McNeal. You would make a good Texas Ranger if you ever have a mind to change careers again."

"I appreciate the vote of confidence, but I'm happy where I am for now."

"This fellow you work for now, Fred, he knows of your gift?"

Jerry nodded. "It's why he hired me."

"You trust him?"

Mostly. "Yes."

"It's good to have people you can trust." Tisdale's voice trailed off as he stared out the window.

Jerry circled around to Tisdale's earlier

comment. "That comment you made about your grandmother... You two didn't get along?"

"The woman was as cold as a fall frost," Tisdale replied. "I was sent to live with her after my parents died. I was twelve at the time, and times as they were, we'd never met. My folks were not of means and didn't have the money to send a boy off on a train. Probably for the best, as my father would speak of her from time to time, but never with any compassion. I am not rightly sure she was even aware of my existence prior to receiving the telegraph letting her know of my folks' death and telling her I was to be sent to the children's home should she not wish to care for me. I'm not sure why she agreed to take me in, and often wished she hadn't, as the woman had no patience. Especially for a rambunctious boy who thought he was old enough to be on his own and who knew things he shouldn't know."

Something about the statement unsettled him. Then it hit him that was the reason for all the questions. Jerry glanced in the mirror and met Tisdale's eye. "You had the gift."

Tisdale laughed a haunting laugh. "Your grandmother called it a gift. Mine called it a curse. I knew of my parents' demise even before anyone came to the schoolhouse to tell me. I'd dreamed of the buggy accident the night before. I told my ma, and she promised to be careful. But in the end, it didn't matter because those dreams always came true. It's how I knew that my grandmother would never accept me and the reason I ran away more times than either of us could count. She always had the authorities come to find me. She was one of those do-gooders who always wanted people of the town to think she could do no wrong." He took off his hat and worried at the brim. "I was fourteen the last time I ran off. I made it two counties over before a lawman found me hiding out in a cemetery. He wanted to know what I was doing there. I lied and told him I was sitting there waiting to die."

Jerry couldn't help interrupting the man. "What were you really doing?"

"I was talking to the man who owned the stone."

"You could see spirits?"

"Can't everyone who is like you and me?"

Jerry shook his head. "No, they can't."

"Well, I could, and I had me a nice conversation with that man. He kept talking even when that lawman found me. He told me if I showed him the strap marks on my back, the lawman wouldn't make me go back home."

"Did you show him?"

"I sure did. I yanked my shirt up, showed him the welts, and told him I'd rather die than go back."

"What'd he say?"

"He said the woman was my grandmother, and she had a right to keep me in line."

"What did you do?"

"What the spirit told me to do. I called the lawman by his first name and said, "Eugene, your father never laid a strap on you, and you turned out just fine. Why would you think a boy needs a strap to grow into a good man?"

"What did he say?"

"He asked how I knew his first name and that his pa had never wooped him. I told him because his pa was standing right there and told me so. I went on to describe his pa right down to the suit they buried him in, and the worry stone Eugene had slipped into his pa's pocket when no one was looking. Then I told him his pa said he should take me home with him. That last part was a lie, but he didn't know. I lived with that man, his wife, and three sons for four glorious years. After that, I followed in his and his father's footsteps and became a man of the law."

"Did he ever find out you lied about him taking you home with him?" Jerry asked.

Tisdale flashed a rare smile. "Not until I met him on this side."

"What did he say?"

The smile grew wider. "He said he would have taken me home anyway."

Chapter Ten

Gunter growled a low growl, pulling Jerry from sleep. A second later, the smell of spiced cedar invaded his nostrils. The hair on the back of his neck stood on end as he opened his eyes to see a man with a wide nose, hooded eyes, and a three-day beard sitting in the chair next to him. A dark aura hung over the spirit. He leaned forward, staring at Jerry with a furrowed brow while puffing away at a gold-banded cigar.

Continuing to growl, Gunter leaned forward on the bed, positioning himself between Jerry and the spirit.

This one's going to be trouble. Jerry sighed. "You know there's no smoking in this hotel."

"It doesn't count if you're the only one who can smell it." The man eyed Gunter, then leaned back in his chair and crossed a leg. He took a puff and exhaled, blowing the smoke directly in Jerry's face. "Cohiba Siglo VI – oh, how I love this cigar. The best part of dying is I can now have one anytime I want, and it doesn't cost me a dime. I used to tap the end on the counter before I lit it to signify another nail going into my coffin. Can you believe that? Fifty bucks a pop for something I thought was going to kill me."

Jerry thought of asking him if that was what put him in the ground, but doing so would break his cardinal rule. Instead, he sat up, placing his feet on the floor. "Whatever you want, it will have to wait until after I have my morning coffee."

"I'm not a man used to waiting," the man snarled.

Gunter leaped in front of the spirit, hackles raised.

Jerry nodded toward the dog. "You get past him, we'll talk. If not, it will have to wait."

Gunter barked a ferocious warning that even had Jerry taking a second glance.

The spirit eyed Gunter and took a puff from his cigar. "Not a bad parlor trick." Though his words held conviction, the spirit's diminishing energy betrayed the man's confidence.

"No trick. Now, if you'll excuse me, I am going to relieve myself and get me a cup of coffee." Jerry stood and turned his back to the spirit as he pulled on his pants. The move was not out of modesty, but to clearly show the spirit he wasn't afraid of him.

"I'll come back," the spirit countered.

"Make it quick. I'm heading out soon," Jerry replied. He turned and found the spirit already gone. Jerry glanced at Gunter. "Thanks for the heads-up on that one. I didn't get a warm and fuzzy feeling from him. Make sure to let me know if he comes back."

Gunter smiled a K-9 smile before jumping on the bed, circling several times, and lowering with a groan.

Jerry smiled. "Are you all right there, old man?"

Gunter responded by rolling onto his back and settling in with his feet in the air.

Jerry chuckled. "Take all the time you need, Dude. I'm going to go to the can, then head down to the lobby to grab a coffee. I think I'll also call April before everyone and his brother join us in the Durango."

Gunter closed his eyes.

***

Jerry took his time at breakfast, lingering over both coffee and his chat with April. He enjoyed those early-morning conversations when her voice was still filled with sleep, and he could easily picture her in bed. He hated saying goodbye, but he needed to get on the road, and it wasn't as easy saying the things couples talk about when he knew the conversation to be less private.

Gunter was still in the same position when he

reentered the room. The dog opened his eyes and rolled onto his side with a groan.

Jerry laughed. "You know, for a ghost, you are one lazy dog."

Gunter growled a soft growl, then curled his lips into a grin.

Jerry spoke to the room. "Hello? If you can hear me, I'm ready to listen." Nothing. That was the thing about spirits – they didn't always keep their word. Sometimes they came back, sometimes they didn't. Either way, he wasn't going to wait around. The spirit had found him once; if he truly needed something, he'd find him again. Jerry picked up his bag and scanned the room for anything he'd missed. "You coming, dog?"

Gunter opened his eyes and closed them once again.

"Suit yourself. Check-out is at eleven. Be gone before housekeeping comes in. My luck, the woman will be able to see you and charge me a pet-cleaning fee." Just as he reached for the doorknob, he heard a dog barking in the hall. Jerry turned and looked at Gunter. "Is there something I should be worried about?"

Gunter's tail thumped against the bed as something scratched against the outer door.

Jerry opened the door to see a beautiful full-sized tricolored collie staring up at him. *That explains why Gunter is so tired.* He searched the hall, then shook his head. "I'd invite you in, but I don't think the old boy could handle it." Jerry started to reach for the collie's collar when he heard heavy footsteps in the hall. He looked to see a teenage boy coming their way holding a leash.

"That's my dog, Mister!" he said as he neared.

Jerry pulled the door closed behind him and held up his hands. "I wasn't trying to steal her. I was just going to check her tags."

"Didn't say you were," the kid said between breaths. "I just didn't want you to let her get away. She slipped out of the door a few hours ago when my dad went to get ice. We've been looking for her ever since. It's crazy: twice, when we found her, she slipped onto the elevator before we could catch her. What kind of dog does that?"

One that has help, Jerry thought. He shrugged. "Yep, that's pretty strange."

"Yeah, Mom was afraid she'd get outside and get herself knocked up. The dog, not my mom. She's in heat. The dog is," he clarified with a snicker. "That's why we didn't leave her at the kennel. Mom was afraid she would get pregnant like happened before. She'll be glad that didn't happen this time."

"I wouldn't be too sure of that, kid."

The color drained from the boy's face. "You've seen another dog?"

"Yep, saw a sorry-looking German shepherd lingering around here a few minutes ago," Jerry said loud enough for Gunter to hear.

"Oh yeah?" The kid bent and connected the leash to the dog's collar. "Come on, Dorie, I'd better get you out of here before he comes back."

Dorie whined, pulling against the leash as the boy led her away.

Jerry turned and saw Gunter's head sticking out the door. "Come on, Romeo, you've had enough fun for the day. I'm not going to leave you here to cause any more trouble than you already have. You can sleep in the Durango."

Gunter emitted a bark as if to say, *Are you going to open the door or what?*

Jerry laughed. "Sorry, pal, you're out of luck. My hotel key is on the nightstand."

Gunter yawned a squeaky yawn and pushed his way through the door.

***

Tisdale was waiting in the front seat of the SUV when they reached it. Gunter disappeared and reappeared in the back seat. Jerry slid into the front and stretched his arm to place his bag behind the seat.

Tisdale pushed his hat back as Jerry shut his door. "You smell like a stale cigar."

Jerry sniffed his shirt. "It's not mine."

"Didn't say it was." Tisdale's voice held an edge.

"I had an unexpected visitor this morning," Jerry said, still feeling the need to explain himself.

"What'd he want?"

Jerry shrugged as he started the Durango and placed it into drive. "No clue. I told him I wasn't talking to him before I had my morning cup of joe. When I came back, he was nowhere in sight."

"Only one man I know that smokes those cigars," Tisdale said without looking at him. "Antonio Maioriello."

While Jerry was sure there were others who smoked that brand, it made sense. It wasn't the first time an entity knew how to find him, the present company included. It was clear his morning visitor wanted to have words with him. It was also clear he hadn't been expecting to encounter Jerry's canine bodyguard. "He has something to say. He'll be back."

"You can count on it," Tisdale agreed. "You know, I had a spirit attach himself to me once. A dandy fellow with a foreign tongue at that."

"What did he want?"

"The Devil if I know. I couldn't understand a word the man said. He was all dressed up and had a saber at his side. To tell you the truth, I thought he was going to run it straight through me."

Jerry lifted a brow. "What'd you do?"

"What do you think I did? I slept with one eye open, which is harder than you think. I was out on the trail, and he'd sit around the campfire and sing the same song over and over again. At least, I think it was the same song. Everything he said sounded the same to me. It was winter, and food was scarce. One night, I went to bed hungry on account it had snowed, and I had to hunker down for a couple of days. I woke the next morning to the smell of rabbit cooking on the spit. I figured I was having me one of the hallucinations I heard tell of. But then I pinched myself and knew I was awake. I looked over at the fire, and sure enough, there was a rabbit cooking over the fire. A big one too. I figured it had to be the dandy because there were no footprints anywhere near the camp. I never saw the fellow again after that. I thought about it enough over the years and figured maybe that was why he was there, to see that I didn't starve to death. That or maybe he didn't know he was dead, and it was his way of thanking me for sharing my fire with him."

Jerry had to admit that while he was used to traveling on his own, traveling with Tisdale wasn't so bad. He enjoyed talking to him and listening to the stories the man had to tell. Tisdale spoke a language Jerry could understand. "Why are you here, Tisdale?"

"Does a man have to have a reason? Maybe I'm just hanging around in case you need something from me."

"Maybe you're full of…"

"Ohhh, a fight. You know, I haven't seen a good one of those in years."

Jerry looked in the mirror to see the pink-haired lady grinning back at him. *Great, this is all I need.*

"Well, if you're going to be like this, I'll just wait at the house." The words had no sooner left her mouth than she disappeared.

Jerry glanced at Tisdale. "I can see where not being able to understand would have its advantages."

Tisdale chuckled. "She's harmless."

"You're saying you know what she wants?"

"Nope."

Jerry waited for him to say more, but he never did.

***

Though Jerry was an experienced driver, he was stunned at the combat driving he met in San Antonio. Even Tisdale grew quiet when vehicle after vehicle darted from one lane to the next, seemingly without worry that someone else might be using that space. By the time he found his exit, his knuckles were white from gripping the steering wheel.

The dash lit up, displaying Fred's name. "I see you made it."

"I'd hold that thought until I actually arrive at my destination," Jerry said, only half kidding.

"Problem?" Fred's voice showed concern.

"Traffic here reminds me of some of the third-world countries I've driven in."

"Construction?"

"No, just the kamikaze driving. I've honestly never seen anything like it. Someone wants a lane, they take it. And getting off the expressway is almost like an afterthought. I've seen so many people taking the exit ramp at the last moment that I've checked half a dozen times to see if I have my blue lights on."

Fred laughed. "You're a Marine. I'm sure you can handle it."

"Maybe so, but my passenger is white as a ghost."

"Your passenger is a ghost," Fred said dryly.

"Oh, yeah, I guess he's okay then." Jerry glanced at the dash. "You know that man you sent me here to find?"

"Antonio Maioriello? What about him?"

"That's the one. I just wanted you to know he's officially dead."

"You sure?"

"Yep. That or there's another entity doing a darn good impersonation of the man's spirit."

"You just got into town. How is it you already found the guy?"

"He found me this morning before I left the hotel."

"What did he want?"

"I don't know."

"You didn't talk to him?"

"Sure, I did. I told him I wasn't going to have a conversation with him until after I had my morning coffee." Jerry waved a hand to get Tisdale's attention and whispered so that Fred couldn't hear. "Here it comes."

"YOU DID WHAT?!" Fred's voice boomed through the dash.

Jerry winked at Tisdale. "You heard me."

"Let me get this straight. I send you to find this man, and he shows up ready to talk, and you tell him you can't be bothered until you have your morning coffee."

"Yep."

"Why?"

"Because a man in my position has to have ground rules."

"I don't believe this."

Jerry smiled. "Have you ever seen the movie *Ghost*? Of course, you have. Everyone has. Do you know that scene when the spirits learn Oda Mae Brown can speak to the dead, and all the spirits were lined up waiting their turn to talk through her?"

"You mean to tell me that's real?"

"I haven't actually had anyone possess me, but I guarantee if I don't set some boundaries, I'll never sleep through the night again if that kind of thing gets around." Jerry looked at Tisdale. "Isn't that right, Clive?"

Tisdale nodded his head.

"You can't see him, but he agreed with me."

"Yeah, well, you better hope you didn't scare the

man off. I've got people breathing down the back of my neck. You better figure out a way to convince Bruno Deluca that Maioriello is dead, or you'll be looking for a new job." The dash cleared, letting Jerry know Fred had ended the call.

Jerry blinked his surprise. Fred had always been intense, but he'd never threatened to fire him before. Jerry glanced at Tisdale. "Was that a threat?"
The ranger nodded his head. "Sounded like a threat to me."

Chapter Eleven

The house Fred put Jerry up in was nondescript. Situated on a corner lot in a well-established subdivision, the home was white-painted brick with black accents and a slightly sloped double driveway leading into an attached garage. Inside, the six-bedroom, six-bath house was another story. Keeping with the black and white theme, the main floor was open concept living, dining, and kitchen, with doors that led to the garage and laundry area. A glass door off the back living room opened into the yard, which housed an inground pool. The yard, which was surrounded by a privacy fence, was not without faults, as the surrounding houses were two stories with windows that allowed their occupants to look down into the backyard.

Jerry looked at the wooden deck attached to a neighboring house. *So much for privacy*. Still, the lounge chairs and covered picnic area would have looked rather inviting if not for the fact it was hotter than blue blazes outside.

Jerry turned and surveyed the two-story living area, admiring the neon green CACTUS CLUB sign, which hung above the gas fireplace. *Nice, maybe we should give our new house a cool name.* He took a photo of the sign and sent it to April along with a text. > *What do you think of giving our new home a cool name?*

April replied. > *I'm open to the idea. What do you have in mind?*

Jerry hadn't expected her to ask his opinion. > *Maybe we should call it the Love Shack.*

April replied with several laughing emojis. He could see she was typing, so he waited for her response, which came a moment later. > *Have you seen the house plans? The house is not going to be a shack. Plus, I doubt Max would feel comfortable going to school telling her friends we've named our house the Love Shack.*

Jerry texted his reply. > *Yeah, I guess I'd better give it some more thought.*

April replied with another laughing emoji. > *I'll give it some thought too. Love you.*

Jerry > *I love you too.*

This time, April replied with a heart. Jerry smiled and pocketed the phone.

Gunter led the way as they went from room to

room, inspecting the house. A bedroom sat near the front door. While it had a king-size bed, it wasn't an en suite, so he closed the door. He found a first-floor master with a king bed and private bath tucked behind the stairs. "This is more like it. You can have the other room; this one is mine. Let's go check out the upstairs."

Jerry placed his bag on the bed and left the room, taking the stairs two at a time. Gunter one-upped him, bypassing the stairs altogether and meeting him at the top of the landing. Jerry leaned down and roughed the dog's fur. "Showoff."

Gunter jumped up, placing his feet on Jerry's chest.

Jerry scratched him behind the ears. "I'm glad you're here. This is a pretty big house for just one person. I guess Fred chose it when he thought April and Max would be joining us."

The hallway was wide, with a plexiglass half wall overlooking the living area below and white walls with black doors on the right. Gunter lowered to the ground and pressed his nose to the clear plexiglass rail, which ran the length of the upper floor. Jerry joined him at the rail. It was easy to see the home could easily accommodate more than him and his ghostly companion. A pang of sadness jolted him. While he was used to working alone, he now wished nothing more than for April and Max to be here to share this experience with him.

Jerry shook off the melancholy and went to work testing the doors on the upper floor. With the exception of a small utility closet, each of the doors revealed an oversized bedroom complete with a king bed. All but one had a full bath.

He opened the door at the end of the hall, blew out a low whistle, and looked at Gunter. "Never mind. You can have the room downstairs. This one is mine."

While the downstairs master was more than adequate, this one was spacious by anyone's standards. It housed a California king bed, two nightstands, a chair and a vanity. The black and white theme carried through in this room with a wall of heavy black curtains behind a black velvet headboard and a pile of black pillows that made him long to have April there even more. *You're not here for a vacation, Marine. You're here to work. The sooner you complete your mission, the sooner you can get home to your family.* Jerry sighed and turned away from the bed.

The closet attached to the room was empty and larger than some of the apartments Jerry had owned, with enough shelves and hanging space to accommodate an entire family. *This thing is nearly as big as my apartment in Chambersburg.*

Returning to the bedroom, he pushed the barn door open to reveal a master bath that easily could have been on the cover of a magazine. With a modern double vanity, black standalone tub, and a glass-enclosed shower large enough to lie down in, the room was beyond impressive at best. The toilet was tucked into a small alcove to the left of the shower.

April would love this place. He took out his phone, took several photos, and sent them to her with a caption that said, *"Wish you were here"*, then waited for her to respond. When she didn't answer, he pocketed his phone.

Gunter was lying crouched on the bed when he came out of the bathroom. Jerry shook his head. "Oh no, you don't. There are five other beds in this place, nearly as big as this one. You go find another. This one's mine!"

Gunter lowered into a playful bow.

"No dice, Dude. I'm not sharing."

Gunter leapt from the bed, raced down the hall, and led the way downstairs. Jerry skirted around the massive island and opened the fridge to find it well-stocked, including a six-pack of beer. *Nice.* Forgoing the beer at the moment, he pulled out a bottle of water, opened it, and drank half. He lifted the bottle in a toast. "Good ole Fred, he thinks of everything."

Jerry reached for his phone to call the man to thank him, recalled their last conversation, and decided against it. Instead, he sat on a stool at the counter, pulled the manila envelope close, and emptied the contents on the counter. Gunter plopped to the floor beside his stool.

Jerry picked up a photo and stared at it. Even without looking at the writing on the back, he knew the picture to be of Antonio Maioriello, as it looked just like the spirit who had woken him earlier this morning. He set the photo aside, lifted another one, and looked at the back. *Bruno Deluca.*

Jerry showed the photo to Gunter. "Yo, dog, take a good look at this man. He's one bad dude. You see him, let me know." Gunter woofed his understanding, then rested his head on his paws as Jerry spent the next few moments sifting through photos and reading over the files.

Gunter leapt to his feet as Jerry stood and stuffed everything back into the envelope. Jerry smiled at the dog. "What say you and I go for a drive?"

Gunter barked and spun in a circle. As they neared the front door, Gunter stopped at the unused bedroom and growled a warning. Jerry opened the door to see the lady with pink hair standing beside the bed, unpacking a small suitcase.

"I hope you don't mind my using this room. It doesn't have a bathroom, not that I need one." The woman smiled. "One of the perks of being dead."

Jerry started to ask where she got the suitcase, then decided against it since he neither cared nor had the time to get into it. "Be my guest." The spirit giggled, and Jerry realized he'd just invited her to stay. He closed the door, exited through the front, and followed as Gunter led the way to the Durango.

Jerry started to program the navigator to the downtown area, then decided against it, opting to let his instincts show him the way. Traffic had died back a bit but still warranted extra caution. He felt the pull tug him in another direction, but knew it wasn't the energy he was originally following. He ignored the new tug, and the urge to follow passed.

Jerry rolled his neck. This was why he disliked large cities – it was easy to get distracted. He followed the original pull onto the interstate, and the energy changed.

Gunter whined.

Jerry knew the dog felt the change. He reached a hand to settle him. "Easy, boy. I feel it too."

Jerry followed his lead and took the exit that led to the Riverwalk. As soon as he exited the highway, Gunter pushed his head through the window as if doing so would help him find what they were looking for.

A minivan pulled away from the curb. *Good deal.* Jerry claimed the parking space and eased the Durango to the curb. He exited, and Gunter glued himself to Jerry's side. The dog was on edge, and Jerry knew better than to think it was merely because they were in an unfamiliar area.

Gunter whipped his head around, growling a warning.

Jerry looked to see what had startled the dog and

relaxed at seeing a pair of park police on bicycles coming up behind them. Jerry sent a silent message to the dog. *It's okay, boy. They're friendly.*

Gunter eased his stance but continued to watch the men as they neared. Jerry returned their greeting as they passed.

They had gone another block when the steady beat of horse hooves filled the air. For a moment, Jerry thought the sound was coming from a ghostly spirit until a horse and carriage came into view from a side street. The horse clopped along at a steady pace while the driver of the carriage regaled the occupants with stories of the area. Jerry was about to look away when he saw a ghostly shadow sitting beside the man. He hurried to catch up and saw Tisdale sitting next to the driver.

Gunter barked as they passed, causing the horse to spook. The driver clicked his tongue and spoke in easy tones as the horse continued a sideways prance past the ghostly K-9. Once the horse settled, Jerry followed, chuckling to himself as the driver proclaimed the horse to have been spooked by the ghost of a woman that sometimes haunted that section of the street. Jerry smiled, knowing Gunter's shenanigans most likely earned the man a better tip.

As Jerry rounded the corner, the sound of hundreds of squeaky toys filled the air. Gunter surged forward, and the night sky filled with birds. Gunter returned to his side, and the flock settled into the neighboring trees, their high-pitched squeaky cries filling the night air once more. Jerry crossed the street, hoping to get a video of the anomaly. As he reached the sidewalk, a woman's screams filled the air. He scanned the area, homing in on the direction of the screams. Even as he felt for the pistol secured in the back waist of his pants, his gift told him the woman wasn't in danger. He left the gun in place as he hurried toward the young woman, who was frantically batting at her shirt.

"It's not funny!" she yelled as the woman standing next to her laughed.

The woman standing beside her giggled. "I've heard that it's good luck if a bird poops on you."

The first woman continued to wipe at the smear with a tissue. "That's an old wives' tale."

Maybe so, but it was something he'd heard Granny say, going further to tell him it was because it rarely happened. Jerry looked to the sidewalk, which was covered in good luck. *Probably doesn't hold true when there are so many birds to contend with.* Either way, he was fairly certain the woman wasn't feeling so lucky at the moment. Jerry offered a weak smile as he passed and decided to forgo trying to video the wayward birds.

"Watch out!" one of the women called after him. "The grackles are out to get us!"

Jerry had heard grackles before, but never had he heard them make this particular noise, nor had he seen so many together in one place. He waved a hand to acknowledge the warning. "Thanks. I'll be sure to keep my head down." He felt the pull within a few steps, following until the sound of horse hooves caught his attention. He looked up expecting to see a horse and carriage but was taken aback at seeing a man dressed solely in white sitting on top of a coal-black horse. The Lone Ranger! Jerry blinked and realized he was seeing an apparition.

The spirit pushed his hat back.

Tisdale. Jerry smiled. "I was wondering where you'd gone off to."

"I had to get my horse."

Gunter moved closer to smell the animal.

A couple came by, holding hands. Jerry pretended to be checking his phone for directions.

The man spoke up. "If you're looking for the Riverwalk, it is just over that bridge and down the steps on the other side."

"Thanks." Jerry pocketed his phone and waited for them to pass. The dog and horse were now nose to nose, checking each other out. Jerry wished he could snap a photo of the ghostly encounter. At least he'd be able to tell April and Max about it later. The moment caught up with him in a wave, and he dearly wished the two were there to share it with him. *Give it a rest, McNeal. You're acting like a lovesick puppy.*

The energy changed, Gunter growled, and the horse reared, his long legs pawing at some unseen threat.

Tisdale held on to the reins as he called out to Jerry. "Heads up, McNeal, there's foul wind brewing!"

A chill raced up Jerry's spine as he recalled the clerk at the store in Deadwood using the same phrase.

Chapter Twelve

Even if Tisdale wasn't leading the way, Jerry wouldn't need to ask for directions. The pull was strong. Jerry jumped when his cell rang announcing April's call. Until that moment, he hadn't realized just how tense he was. He started to answer, saw that Gunter was wearing his police vest and knew he wasn't the only one on edge. He debated ignoring the call but knew doing so would only cause April to worry, especially if Max had picked up on his energy. He swiped to answer. "You good?"

"Of course."

"Then can I call you back?"

"Are you good?" Though the last thing he wanted to do was worry her, her tone showed he'd done just that.

Jerry worked to keep his voice light. "I'm good. Just following a lead and need to…"

"Do what you do," she said, cutting him off. "Go ahead. Call me when you can."

"It might be late."

"It's already late. I won't be able to sleep unless you let me know you're safe."

"I'm with Gunter and Tisdale. I couldn't be any more safe than I am right now," Jerry replied, hoping it to be true.

"Please."

"Yes, ma'am."

"Oh, Max wanted me to tell you to check out the basement."

"Basement? Has she been watching Pee Wee Herman?"

April laughed. "Not that I know of. Why do you ask?"

"Because the Alamo doesn't have a basement. It was a scene in a Pee Wee movie and I'm sure it's a running joke around here."

"Maybe so. But I didn't get the impression Max was kidding. She specifically said, 'Make sure Jerry checks the basement.' Maybe there's a basement in the house you're staying in?"

"Nope."

"Okay, I'll let her know. But if you go anywhere that has a basement, be sure to check it out."

"Will do."

Gunter growled and moved in front of Jerry.

Not wishing to further worry her, Jerry kept the

tension out of his voice. "Hey, I've got to go."

"Okay, love you."

"Love you too." As he ended the call, a woman's screams filled the air. Only this time, the sound caused the hair on Jerry's neck to stand on end.

Tisdale leaned forward, and the phantom horse took off like something was chasing it. Gunter sprinted forward, stopped to make sure Jerry was following, then turned, following the horse and rider into the night. Jerry ran after them, but even though he'd gotten back into a running routine, found he was no match for the speed of his ghostly companions. He ran west on E. Commerce Street, and even before the pull had him taking a right onto Alamo Plaza, knew he was heading to the Alamo.

The woman's screams had evolved into sobs by the time he reached her. Jerry wasn't sure if it was because park police had arrived before him or because Tisdale's and Gunter's spirits stood guard over her as she recounted her story to the two officers. The group was standing in the shadow of a statue of a woman holding a child, which seemed rather fitting, since the woman looked to be in the later stages of pregnancy.

"I think it was a ghost," she said just as Jerry neared.

One of the officers looked in his direction, appraised him briefly, and motioned him to move along. Jerry debated arguing the point but didn't want to face confrontation just yet – especially not after the woman had just proclaimed to have been accosted by a ghost. If he were to produce his credentials, jokes would ensue, and the last thing he wanted was to make a mockery of the fact that the woman was obviously terrified.

Jerry moved away but stayed within earshot of the small group. Holding up his phone, he played tourist, taking photos of the historical structure to share with his family later. As the woman spoke, he surveyed Alamo Square. Floodlights in front of the cream-colored building created shadows on the stone fortress and made for an eerie setting against the night sky. *Maybe she's heard one too many ghost stories.* Jerry resisted a chuckle. *Why so cynical, McNeal? Do you think you hold the patent on seeing ghosts?* Of course, he didn't, but it was also true that most of the time people claimed to have seen a ghost, they were either making it up, or the supposed sighting could be explained. *Not today.* Of course, just because the pull was real didn't mean her story was. While he knew she was telling the truth as she knew it, it didn't necessarily make her attacker a ghost. He searched the shadows for anything amiss. *Nothing.* He moved closer, pretending to photograph the statue near where they stood.

"I'm telling you, I was standing here waiting for my husband to bring the car around. We've been walking all day; these are new shoes and I have blisters," she said by way of explanation. "That's it. I was just standing here, and someone grabbed me."

The taller of the two park officers took the lead. "And you didn't get a look at the person who grabbed you?"

She shook her head. "No, I already told you. He grabbed me from behind."

"Are you sure it was a man?" the officer asked.

"I'm sure. I didn't see him, but he was too strong to be a woman."

"Women can be strong," the officer interjected. "Since you didn't get a good look…"

"It was a man. I felt the stubble of his beard, and when he spoke, he smelled like a stale cigar."

Her comment had Jerry moving closer.

"Do you know which way he ran?" the officer asked.

"No. I screamed, and when I turned around, there was no one there. I know there are things he could have hidden behind, but I'm telling you, he wouldn't have had time." She sniffed, her eyes darting from side to side. "I know it sounds crazy, but it's like he just disappeared into thin air."

The two officers exchanged glances, but there were no dismissive smirks.

They believe her. Jerry rocked back on his heels, going over the implications in his mind.

Tisdale moved to his side. "This isn't the first incident," the spirit said, confirming his thoughts. "I overheard the officers talking as they arrived. They probably won't admit it, but they're spooked. It all started around the same time Maioriello started showing up in photos."

Gunter turned his attention toward the landmark, ears erect and twitching like antennas.

"I'll get Fred to get me inside the Alamo so I can take a look," Jerry whispered. Jerry pulled up Fred's number and typed, > *I need to get into the Alamo.*

The reply was instant. >*When?*

Jerry hit reply. > *Right now.*

A few seconds passed before Fred sent another message. > *Hang tight. The cavalry's on the way.*

Jerry was about to type a witty response about them not saving the Alamo the first time, when Gunter barked and took off toward the stone building, leaping and disappearing through the arched wooden doorway. Jerry looked at Tisdale.

"I'm on it." Tisdale had no sooner said the words than he, too, disappeared.

Laughter filled Alamo Plaza, though he was the only one who seemed to notice. Jerry turned to see Antonio Maioriello leaning against a tree some distance away.

The energy around the spirit was as dark as the night sky surrounding him. "Like taking candy from a baby. Make a little ruckus inside, and all your defenses disappear. Seriously, they warned me you were coming and said I should be worried. I thought you were supposed to be something, but you're no different than the rest."

Jerry glanced at the park police.

Maioriello laughed a haunting laugh. "What? Do you expect them to shoot me?"

Jerry blocked the spirit from reading his thoughts and pulled himself taller. "You're wrong, Maioriello, I wasn't looking at them for help. I wanted to make sure they weren't going to stop me. That's right, I know who you are," Jerry said when Maioriello's face turned serious.

"Yeah, then you know what I can do to a person like you," Maioriello said, pushing away from the tree.

Gunter, I could use a little help out here.

Maioriello moved closer.

Gunter, I need help!

Instantly, Gunter was at his side, snarling and barking.

A whistle pierced the air, and Maioriello disappeared.

"That is not okay!"

Jerry turned to see who was shouting, surprised to see one of the park police officers heading his way.

Face devoid of any humor, the man closed the distance with a determined stride.

Gunter turned and focused his attention on the man, barking a warning.

"Why isn't that dog on a leash?" the man asked heatedly.

Because I didn't think you could see him. Think, Jerry. Give Fred time to do his thing. Jerry looked at the man's nametag. *Murphy.* "Because we're working. We heard the screams and came to see if we could help." He palmed a hand in front of Gunter's face. "Easy, boy, Officer Murphy is not the enemy."

The barking stopped, but Gunter continued to emit a low growl.

Jerry studied the officer, knowing Gunter only reacted when he felt Jerry was in danger.

Murphy wasn't deterred. "I don't know who you think you are, but this is my jurisdiction. We just had a woman assaulted. You wouldn't know anything about that, would you?"

Jerry rubbed a hand across his chin. "I'm not your guy unless you think I shaved and showered in the last ten minutes."

Murphy frowned. "Yeah, maybe not. Get that pup on a leash before I cite you and call animal control to pick him up."

Pup? Jerry glanced at Gunter. *Houdini? What the…* "Houdini, heel!" Instantly, Houdini fell into position beside Jerry. While the growling stopped, the pup's hackles stood on end as he now focused his attention on Maioriello, who was just slipping through the front door of the Alamo. Not wanting the spirit to get away, Jerry started to reach for his badge.

Murphy's hand hovered above his holster. "Hands where I can see them!"

Way to go, McNeal. Keep this up and you're going to get yourself shot. Jerry lifted his hand. "I need to get into the Alamo."

"It opens at 9."

"I didn't ask you what time it opens. I said I need to get inside," Jerry said coolly.

Houdini barked.

Jerry kept his fingers spread as he lowered a hand in front of the pup's face. "Easy, boy." Jerry met Murphy's eye and lowered his voice. "I wasn't going to draw on you. I was going to show my badge."

Murphy raised an eyebrow. "You're a cop?"

"Used to be. My name's Jerry McNeal. I'm the Lead Paranormal Investigator for the Department of Defense here on special assignment."

"Sure, buddy, and I'm Superman. If you were here on assignment, don't you think I'd know about it? How much have you had to drink tonight?" Murphy asked, taking a step.

Houdini moved in front of Jerry, baring his teeth.

"I'm not drunk, and I do have a badge. And unless you want to tangle with the dog, you'll take a step back."

The officer hesitated and called his partner. "Hey, Lewis, does the DOD have a Lead Paranormal

Investigator working in the area?"

"A what?"

"That's what I thought." Murphy reached for his taser. As he pulled it free, Gunter appeared out of nowhere, knocking the man to the ground and standing over him. From the bewildered look on the man's face, it was clear he had no clue how he got taken down.

Jerry held his hands up as Lewis pulled his weapon. "You really don't want to do that."

"McNeal's right, Lewis, he's not doing this. He was nowhere near me when it hit me."

Gunter, let that man up. You started this. How about a little help?

Gunter pranced over to Lewis as if this was all a glorious game. He placed his paws on the man's chest and panted in the man's face.

Houdini whined, as if wanting to join in on the fun, but ultimately stayed at Jerry's side.

"W-what's going on here?" Lewis stammered. "I swear there's someone breathing in my face."

Jerry took control. "The woman was telling the truth. She was attacked by a spirit, but you already know that because this isn't the first time. That's why the government sent me."

Murphy stood and brushed himself off. He glanced in the direction where the woman now stood with the man she'd been waiting for. "Only one problem. We've been told to keep this under wraps.

What do we tell the lady?"

"The same thing you'd tell her if her attacker had been flesh and blood. Take her statement, get her contact information, and tell her you'll be in touch if there are any developments."

Murphy nodded to Lewis, who seemed pleased to be excused as he nearly ran to where the couple stood.

"Now what?" Murphy asked.

Jerry looked to the Alamo and sighed. "Now we wait."

"Wait for what?"

"The cavalry."

"You realize the irony of that comment, don't you?"

Jerry nodded.

Houdini followed Gunter's lead and lowered into a crouch.

Murphy motioned toward Houdini. "What's with the leash?"

Jerry followed his gaze. "What leash?"

Murphy sighed. "That's kind of my point. There are leash laws. Why isn't he wearing one?"

"His name's Houdini," Jerry said by way of explanation. "He hasn't met a harness he can't get out of." Both dogs barked. Jerry looked up to see two black SUVs pull to the curb.

Eight men dressed solely in black filed out, heading in their direction. As they walked under the lamppost, Jerry realized both Fred and Barney were leading the charge.

"The cavalry?" Murphy asked.

"Yep," Jerry replied.

"They don't look like much."

Jerry smiled. "They're enough."

The duo stopped, pointed, and barked orders as four men took positions around the courtyard and stood watching the perimeter. Two escorted a smaller man who looked as if he'd been pulled out of bed directly to the front door of the Alamo. Fred stopped short, obviously waiting for Jerry to join him. Barney walked directly to Murphy, flashing his credentials.

Gunter and Houdini followed as Jerry walked to where Fred was standing. Houdini stayed next to Jerry, sniffing the air, while Gunter moved in for a more personal greeting.

Oblivious to Gunter's advances, Fred studied Houdini. "This the ghost pup?"

Jerry nodded.

Fred held out his hand, smiling as Houdini stretched his neck to sniff the offering. "How come I can see him?"

"He's only half ghost," Jerry reminded him.

Fred nodded. "I thought you said he went back home."

"He did. Showed up again a few minutes ago."

Fred lifted a brow. "Showed up?"

"Maioriello made an appearance, but not before causing a distraction and luring Gunter and Tisdale away."

Reminded of the problem at hand, Fred scanned the courtyard. "Is Maioriello still here?"

Jerry shook his head. "No, he left when the police got involved."

Fred's gaze settled on the building. "You said you need to get inside. You think he's in there?"

"He seems to be haunting this area. If he's not out here, there's a good chance he's in there." Jerry thought about what April had said about the basement and kicked at the stone sidewalk with the toe of his shoe.

"Okay, McNeal, I've known you long enough. What's on your mind?"

Not having a choice, Jerry pushed forward with the question at hand. "Don't laugh, but I need to know once and for all if there's a basement under the Alamo."

For the first time since Jerry had known him, Fred cut loose with a full belly laugh.

"What's so funny?" Barney asked, joining them.

Fred jutted his chin toward Jerry. "The kid here has been watching too many movies."

Barney smiled. "Let me guess, he wants to know if there is a basement in the Alamo."

Fred laughed once more.

"Go ahead and laugh," Jerry said dryly. "I know

there's no basement, but Max keyed on it, so I had to ask."

"Max is pulling your leg." Fred chuckled.

Barney held up a finger, wagging it back and forth. "Not so fast, old wise one."

Fred stilled. "Barney, you know as well as I there is no basement under the Alamo."

Barney nodded his agreement. "True, but there is one under the gift shop, which is but a few feet away. If Max is picking up on a basement, perhaps that's the one."

As soon as he said it, Jerry knew it was the one. He looked at Fred. "Can you get me in there?"

Fred whipped out his phone. "Consider it done."

Chapter Thirteen

Gunter and Houdini heeled beside Jerry as he walked across the plaza to meet the man with the key, who was introduced as a Mr. Livingston. The man's brow furrowed when being introduced, giving Jerry the distinct feeling that it wasn't his real name. That, or the guy wasn't supposed to have a key to the building in the first place and didn't appreciate being outed.

Jerry went along with the charade, knowing if Fred was shielding him from any wrongdoing, it was best to keep his head in the sand. The man opened the door to the Alamo and waved a hand.

Fred shook his head. "Change of plans; we need to get into the basement."

Jerry started to tell Fred there was no "we," but decided it best to fight that battle when the time came.

Livingston's beady eyes bugged. "The Alamo doesn't have a basement."

"No, but the Alamo gift shop does." Fred's tone left no room for objection.

Livingston pulled the heavy door closed and turned on his heels. "Follow me."

Arriving at the entrance to the gift shop, Fred and Barney once again shielded the man as he worked to unlock the door.

Jerry smiled a knowing smile. "He doesn't really have a key, does he?" *Way to go, McNeal. So much for keeping your head in the sand.*

Fred matched his smile. "Ask me again and I'll tell you."

Barney clamped a hand on Jerry's shoulder. "You don't want to go down that rabbit hole, McNeal. It will take you on a trip you might not be prepared for."

Jerry looked Barney in the eye. "What the heck is that supposed to mean?"

Barney leaned in and lowered his voice to a whisper. "I was once blindly happy. Now, I question everything."

"You work for the government, and you're telling me you're a conspiracy theorist?"

Barney leaned closer. "I'm telling you that working for the government makes me want to question everything."

Jerry raised an eyebrow. "Does the agency

know?"

Barney's lips curved into a sly smile. "What agency?"

"*Voila*!" Livingston said, holding the door open for all to enter.

"Curses, foiled again," Barney said, then turned and followed the others inside.

Fred hung back and moved alongside Jerry as he passed. "Don't mind Barney; he didn't have many friends when he was little."

"Sounds familiar," Jerry quipped. Gunter edged Houdini aside to move in closer. Jerry reached a hand to his K-9 partner. *Thanks, buddy. I love you too.* Jerry caught Fred looking, started to remove his hand, then decided against it.

The procession stopped at a door marked "employees only." Livingston knelt and worked to unlock it.

Jerry moved forward and turned to face the others. "I'll have you all wait here."

"That's not the deal," Fred protested.

"The deal," Jerry said, matching Fred's tone, "is you brought me here to do a job."

Fred leveled his gaze at Jerry. "Bruno is in town. You don't tie this up soon and he's going to send his men into the Alamo guns blazing."

"Then either close the building to tourists or stand back and let me do what you hired me to do."

"The master bested by the student," Barney

quipped.

Jerry shook his head. "I'm not trying to best anyone. The simple truth of the matter is our friend is not going to show himself if I show up with an entourage."

Fred moved to the side. "Okay, McNeal, but for the record, I don't like you going down there alone."

"While I appreciate your concern, we both know an arsenal wouldn't help me." Jerry motioned the dogs forward. "Besides, I'm not going alone. I have the dogs."

Livingston furrowed his brow. "Dogs? What dogs? I only see one."

"Don't believe everything you see," Barney quipped.

"Were you talking to him or me?" Jerry asked.

Barney handed him a flashlight. "Go forth and conquer, brave knight."

Jerry pocketed the flashlight and turned on the light switch leading down the stairs. Though he'd thought Fred to be kidding at the time, he was now beginning to think there was something truly off with Barney.

He felt the pull the second his foot touched the first stair and knew without a doubt, Max had steered him in the right direction. As he descended the basement stairs, the dogs' throaty growls confirmed that thought. Instead of retreating, he hurried downward to see what had the dogs so riled.

As he suspected, the basement served as a storage room for giftshop overflow with long rows of shelving housing box after box of merchandise. Jerry followed both the pull and continued growls, searching each row as he crept along the room's outer edge. As he reached the last row, he saw Tisdale and a spirit he'd not seen before standing over Maioriello. Maioriello's spirit had a cloth stuffed in his mouth and was bound with a thick brown rope. He sat on what looked like an old milk crate, staring up at him as if he didn't have a care in the world. Gunter and Houdini flanked both lawmen, hackles raised as if daring the criminal to try and escape.

Tisdale gave a nod. "Bout time you showed up. We caught the varmint some minutes ago. Raymond here wanted to haul him away, but I thought maybe you'd need to talk to him."

"Raymond? You're the ranger?" The question was a mere matter of formalities since the man was wearing a white shirt and hat and wore a tin star on his chest.

Raymond nodded.

Jerry wasn't sure what to make of the situation, especially since he had so many questions. Like, how did they find a rope to hold the guy when he'd yet to figure out how to detain Houdini? And where exactly would they be taking him? The man was dead. Even before that, he'd made a deal with the law preventing him from serving time. Were such deals not honored on the other side?

"We Texas Rangers are dedicated to the star," Tisdale said, reading his mind once more. "Raymond here was this fellow's chaperone and doing a good job before they were both killed. He may be dead, but he gave an oath to protect the man, and that's what he intends to do."

Jerry looked at Raymond. "Protect him from who, and how is hogtying him protecting him?"

Raymond spoke up. "We're protecting him from some of Bruno's men who are walking on this side. They know the big guy's upset and plan on making amends. It all started when Maioriello started making a spectacle of himself."

Jerry rubbed a hand over his head. "He's dead. Doesn't that count for anything?"

Raymond nodded. "Most of the time. When we died, that should have been the end of it, but he chose to further antagonize the fellows that he informed against. In turn, that set off a domino effect where those fellows are making threats to our fellow rangers. We are family, and you don't treat the star like that. I was going to take him somewhere until things settle down, but Clive didn't think that would be the end of things, so he insisted on finding someone to help."

Jerry nodded his understanding. "That someone being me."

Tisdale spoke up. "I'd heard about you and knew you would be able to help. Apparently, I was right because I had nothing to do with them sending you here."

Jerry stepped closer, and both dogs took up positions at each side. "Tisdale's right. Giving Maioriello the bum's rush out of here isn't going to accomplish anything. I need you to remove the gag so I can have a conversation with him."

Raymond addressed Maioriello. "This nice young man wishes to have a word with you. Keep your tongue civil, or the gag goes back in, got it?"

Maioriello nodded.

Raymond removed the cloth and looked at Jerry. "Go on with your questions, son."

Jerry leaned over Maioriello. "You know I know who you are. I also know about the deal you made to get you into WITSEC."

"Then you know I went into witness protection for nothing. Bruno's guys found me and offed me anyway."

Actually, Jerry hadn't known that until a few moments ago. Neither did Fred, or it would have been in the report. Jerry covered his thoughts. "There's a reason you're haunting the Alamo. What is it?"

"Because Bobby the Bull's niece, Maria Carmichael, works here."

Jerry shrugged. "Who is this Bobby guy, and

why do you care about his niece?"

"Bobby is the guy who offed us," Maioriello said. "He doesn't have a daughter, so I figured I'd make it tough on his niece. She's his sister's kid. Bobby's her godfather."

"You're dead. Why not just wash your hands of the whole mess?" Jerry asked.

"I was okay with that until I decided to check in on my family – you know, just to tell them one last goodbye – and I saw Bruno and his boys sitting on my couch. Can you believe that? Bruno knows I ratted on him, so the only explanation is he was trying to get payback for me squealing on him."

Something wasn't adding up. "You were there. Didn't you hang around to see what was said?"

Maioriello glanced at Houdini. "No, my wife has this little mutt and it turns out dogs can see us. He kept yapping at me and yapping, so I decided to come back later to ask. Only when I came back, the dog could see me, but my wife couldn't."

"Bruno's got a family. He ordered the hit. Why not bug them? Why pick on Bobby's niece?"

"Because she's the only one who can see me. At first, I thought she knew I was dead, but maybe not, because she told them I was there but never said I was dead."

Jerry smiled as the pieces of the puzzle fell into place.

"What's with the stupid grin? I thought you came

here to fix this mess?"

Jerry's smile grew. "I did, and I will."

"Cool, let's go."

Jerry shook his head. "No deal. I'll bring Bruno to you."

"The man's an animal. How are you going to get him to agree to that?"

"You let me worry about that." Jerry looked at Tisdale. "You guys good hanging out here a bit longer?"

Tisdale slid his hat back. "I've got an eternity."

"Good to know, but if my plan works, this shouldn't take that long." Jerry turned on his heels and raced up the stairs.

Fred looked past him. "Where's the dog?"

"On guard duty. I don't have a lot of time to explain, but I need you to bring Bruno here. I also need you to find one Maria Carmichael and get her here too."

Fred shook his head. "I can probably get you Maria, but no way Bruno's going to go for it."

Jerry chuckled. "You're telling me the great Alfred Jefferies can't work his magic to prevent another attack on the Alamo?"

Fred held firm. Looking at Barney, he pointed a finger. "Not a word."

Barney clamped his finger to thumb and ran them across his lips. "Consider them zipped."

Jerry sighed. *Think, McNeal. There has to be a*

way. "Fabel!"

Fred frowned. "I know you two are pals, but are you trying to start a turf war?"

"We're far from pals, but Fabel thinks he owes me one. Besides, this is not their turf. They would be meeting on neutral ground."

Fred nodded his agreement. "Okay, McNeal, float your theory."

"I don't need Fabel here. I just need Bruno to think he's coming. Fabel calls up Bruno and tells him he has information on Maioriello and tells him to meet him in the basement at the Alamo. Everyone knows there's no basement at the Alamo, but Bruno's going to want to know what the guy's up to. To sweeten the pot, we'll have Maria leave a cryptic message for her uncle Bobby, telling him Maioriello promised to leave her alone if she can finagle peace talks. Bobby tells that to Bruno, and Bruno will agree to meet with Fabel to learn what he knows."

"How are we going to get Maria to agree to making the call?"

"We don't need Maria to make the actual call. A female who sounds a little like her, along with some static, should do the trick."

"If we're fabricating her voice, why do we need her here at all?"

"Because we do!" Jerry blew out a breath. "I don't have time to explain every little detail, but she needs to be here for this to all work. Just get her here before Bruno arrives. I'll make the call to Fabel and have him tell Bruno to meet him here in an hour." Jerry started to walk away, then hesitated. "Tisdale and the dogs have everything under control. You need to get your team out of here."

"If that man's coming here, my guys aren't going anywhere," Fred countered. Bruno's men will have real guns with real bullets."

Jerry knew he wasn't going to win this one. "Then get them out of sight. Bruno even sniffs a setup, and he's going to be in the wind."

"You're right. The guy's sharp. Much too sharp to walk into a trap. There's no way he's going to agree to go into a basement where there's only one way out."

Jerry closed his eyes. *Good one, McNeal. You can't see the forest for the trees.* He opened his eyes once more. "We don't need the basement. I was just thinking of using that place since Maioriello is already there. These guys with you, you trust them to see and hear things?"

"They wouldn't be here if I didn't," Fred assured him.

"Then we do it right here, right out in the open. Even if Fabel tells Deluca to come alone, he's going to have his guys nearby. Tell your guys to settle in and keep a low profile unless I call in the cavalry."

Barney spoke up for the first time since pretending to zip his lips. "I see what you did there, it being the Alamo and all."

Jerry looked at Fred. "I think Barney's off his meds."

"He's been on assignment and hasn't had much sleep the last couple of days. You take care of Fabel and I'll take care of the rest." He wrapped his arm around Barney's shoulders. "Come on, Barnaby, we'll get you some coffee."

Chapter Fourteen

Jerry stood waiting with his ghostly menagerie for Maria Carmichael to arrive. While standing in the center of the Alamo courtyard made them an open target for anyone looking to take them out, it also provided Fred's snipers a clear shot if Bruno decided to make a move. Jerry knew Maria had arrived even before the dogs alerted him to the girl's arrival.

She was alone, meaning one of Fred's men had let her out a couple of blocks from the square to avoid being seen if Deluca had men watching the square. Houdini inched forward and returned to Jerry's side when Gunter cut him off.

Maria saw him standing next to Maioriello, who was still imprisoned with ropes and gag, and scrunched up her face. That she didn't take off in a panic at the sight of him showed she was well-accustomed to the family lifestyle. "Who are you, and why is Antonio cinched up like that?"

Jerry had given this question a great deal of thought. He was already on one mobster's radar and didn't want to chance Bruno Deluca coming after him or the ones he cared about. "My name isn't important, and these ropes are for all of our protection."

She ran a hand through her dark hair as if considering how much to tell him. "Did he tell you he's been stalking me?"

While Jerry would have preferred to ease into the conversation, he knew time was of the essence. He cut to the chase, knowing he had to get Maria on his side before Bruno arrived. "He's not been stalking you. He's been haunting you."

While the sight of a man hogtied and gagged hadn't affected her, Maria now looked like a rabbit about to bolt. "What do you mean, haunting me?"

Gunter growled, signaling Bruno had arrived. Jerry knew it was too late to bring her to his side. *Okay, boys,* Jerry said silently. *We're going to have to wing it. For all our sakes, let's hope this works.*

Having seen photos of the guy, Bruno Deluca was exactly what Jerry had expected, right down to the single eyebrow and hooded eyes. Even though it was pushing three in the morning, the man wore an expensive suit and walked with a swagger that said, *Mess with me, and I'll have you fitted for concrete boots and toss you in the river myself.* Only from what Jerry had read, Bruno didn't like getting his hands dirty. He preferred his men to do the dirty work. Jerry counted on that to be his way of clearing up this mess without anyone else getting hurt.

Bruno approached, saw Jerry standing next to Maria, and glared at the girl. "Did you set me up?"

Maria blinked her surprise. "No, I would never…"

"Then what's with the fed?"

Dressed in jeans, a black t-shirt, and tennis shoes, Jerry felt he looked nothing like a federal agent, but that Deluca had been in the business so long and remained a free man meant he could sniff out threats.

Jerry held up his hands and pulled up his shirt. "I'm not a fed, and I'm not wearing a wire."

"Yeah, well, I give my guys the go, and I guess it really doesn't matter what you are because you won't be talking to anyone."

"And if anything happens to me, my dog will rip you to shreds before anyone can stop him," Jerry warned.

Bruno chuckled. "That pup? You're kidding, right?"

Gunter moved forward and took Bruno's hand in his mouth.

Maria gasped.

Bruno tried unsuccessfully to pull his hand away. "What the—?"

"My dog," Jerry replied.

Bruno's eyes bugged. "The only dog I see is over there. What kind of game are you playing?"

Maria's face paled. "What do you mean he's over there? He's standing there with your arm in his mouth!"

"Who is?"

"THE DOG!" Maria's eyes were wide with alarm.

"Give your men the signal to stand down, and I'll call off the dog," Jerry said as the feeling of dread washed over him.

"What if I tell them to shoot you instead?"

Jerry shrugged. "Sure thing, if you don't mind joining me on the other side. I'm sure Maioriello would love to have a chat with you."

Bruno lifted his free hand. A second later, the feeling of dread lifted. "They're standing down. Now, stop whatever you're doing here and tell me what Maioriello has to do with this."

Jerry snapped his fingers, and Gunter released Bruno's arm.

Bruno caressed his hand with the other and turned to Maria. "Listen, kid, it's way too early in the morning for theatrics. I don't know what scheme the two of you have concocted, but I came here to meet with Maioriello, so tell me where he is."

Maria blinked her surprise. "You mean to tell me you can't see him?"

Bruno looked about the courtyard. "Of course not. He's not here."

"But, Uncle Bruno, he is. I can see him standing right there."

"I'm not your uncle. Not today."

Tears welled in Maria's eyes. "But I've called you that ever since I was a little girl."

Jerry gave a nod, and Raymond pulled the cloth out of Maioriello's mouth. "Better jump in here, Maioriello. What's it going to take to convince him?"

"Maria. Can you hear me?"

The girl looked directly at Maioriello. "Of course, I can hear you. Why can't he see you?"

"Because I'm dead."

"What do you mean you're dead?"

Bruno started to leave and Gunter stepped in front of him. Bruno wrinkled his brow. "What the…?"

"It's the dog," Maria said.

"Enough with the dog already," Bruno fumed.

"Then leave," Jerry coaxed.

"I can't."

"Tell Bruno I know it was Bobby the Bull who offed me."

"Who told you that?" Bruno asked when Maria repeated what he'd said. "Bobby?"

"No, Uncle Bobby has never talked about Antonio, and I've never asked. Antonio told me himself. He's standing right here."

Maioriello described what happened in great detail, further telling the name of the other man with him while Maria repeated everything word for word. He then told about another incident, giving detailed accounts of what was said. Maria swallowed and repeated those words as well.

Bruno's head jerked up. "He and I were the only ones who knew about that."

"That's what Antonio said."

Bruno's face paled. He narrowed his eyes at Jerry. "What's your part in all of this?"

"I'm a psychic. I can see and speak to the dead. Just like Maria here. The only difference is she didn't know she could do it until a few moments ago."

"What does Maioriello have to do with any of this besides being dead?"

"He was there when you went to his house and spoke to his wife."

"I was paying my respects," Bruno argued.

Jerry rocked back on his heels. "By taking the man who'd killed her husband with you?"

Bruno shrugged. "I wanted him to see her face. A man kills another man, it means something. I needed him to know his actions had consequences."

Jerry arched a brow. "You ordered the hit."

"I did no such thing. Bobby's the one who took it upon himself to off the guy."

Jerry knew Bruno was only saying this so as not to implicate himself. He also now knew where the problem lay. "You might have gone there originally to pay your respects, but you visited again after Maioriello started showing up in photos."

Maioriello started to say something, and Raymond stuck the cloth back into his mouth.

"Your beef isn't with the government," Jerry continued. "It was with your men who told you Maioriello was no longer an issue. When Maioriello started showing up, you thought your men couldn't be trusted. You were worried about a coup. No one is trying to force you out. Your men did exactly what you told them to do. The only problem is they took out the ranger who was watching over him in the process. Raymond Hale is here now, and he is none too happy about being caught up in things."

Bruno looked at Maria.

Maria nodded her head and pointed to Tisdale and Raymond. "He's telling the truth. There are two other men here."

Jerry took a step forward. "You're going to leave Texas and you won't be making any more contact with any of the rangers who worked the case or their families. Got it?"

Bruno laughed, but the humor didn't reach his eyes. "I don't hold too well to threats. I might not know who you are, but I have ways of finding out, and when I do..."

Gunter jumped up, placing his paws on the man's chest, breathing hot air into Bruno's face.

Bruno turned white, and Jerry smiled. "My name's not important, Mr. Deluca. You come after me, the rangers, or even threaten Mario Fabel for setting up this little meeting, and I'll see you pay, whether it be in this life or the next. What is that saying people like you are so fond of saying, an eye for an eye?" *Gunter, down*.

Gunter lowered to the ground, circling Jerry and moving up beside Houdini. As he did, both Tisdale and Raymond appeared on either side of Bruno, pressing their shoulders against the man in what must have felt like a ghostly vise.

Jerry narrowed his eyes at Bruno. "You might have friends among the living, but I have connections your mind wouldn't even begin to fathom. There is no place you can hide that me or my friends can't find you. Anyone I care about so much as trips for an unexplained reason, and I'll assume it was you or one of your men."

Sweat trickled down Bruno's face. "I get the message. Call off the dog."

Jerry smiled an easy smile. "The dog's over here, Bruno. Those are some of my other friends."

Maria bobbed her head. "He's telling the truth, Uncle Bruno. Those men have stars on their chests. I thought they were real Texas Rangers. I didn't know they were ghosts."

"They are real Texas Rangers," Jerry confirmed. "They're just continuing their work on the other side."

Both rangers stepped away from Bruno and tipped their hats to Jerry.

Bruno's shoulders slumped, and he looked very much like a bully who'd just got what was coming to him. After a full moment, he pulled himself taller. "Me and the boys will be leaving town if you don't have any objections."

Jerry worked to keep from smiling. "Am I to understand that you have concluded your business here in San Antonio?"

Bruno nodded. "We have."

"Then I bid you a safe journey," Jerry said sincerely.

Bruno glanced at Maria. "Would you like a ride home?"

Maria's shoulders relaxed. "Yes, Uncle."

That Jerry didn't get a bad feeling as they turned to walk away let him know Bruno meant her no harm.

Jerry turned to where Tisdale and Raymond stood next to Maioriello. "What now?"

Tisdale spoke up. "We're going to keep him tied up until we are certain things have cooled off."

Jerry couldn't resist asking the question. "Actually tied up or busy?" His cell rang, showing Fred's call. Before he got his answer, Tisdale and

Raymond tipped their hats and disappeared, taking Maioriello with them. Houdini barked and sniffed the spot where the trio had previously stood.

"You let Bruno leave. I'm assuming it's done?" Fred said when Jerry answered.

"If you're asking if we saved the Alamo, I believe it's safe to say yes. Bruno and his men are headed out of town as we speak."

"You trust him to keep his word?"

"I do."

"Did you get anything we can use to make sure his departure is permanent?"

"You tell me. I know you were listening the whole time," Jerry replied.

"Feel like getting a coffee and discussing what was said?"

"I feel like getting a shower and hitting the sack." Jerry looked at his phone to check the time and saw he had three missed calls from April. "Crap."

"Problem?"

"I was supposed to call April hours ago. She's probably worried sick right now."

"Relax, McNeal. She called me when you didn't answer her calls."

"What'd you tell her?"

"I told her you were working and assured her that Barney and I are both here. That seemed to settle her."

"I'm glad you spoke to her instead of Barney. He

seemed a little squirrely tonight."

"Just remember, he might seem a little out there at times, but in the end, the guy has your back."

Jerry yawned. "I'm going back to the house, taking a much needed shower and going to bed. When's check-out?"

"The house is one of ours. We don't have anything pressing. Stay there as long as you like."

"I appreciate your offer, but I'm just going to catch some sleep and head out." Jerry slapped his leg for the dogs to follow and started toward his Durango.

"Something wrong with the house?" Fred asked, keeping pace.

"It's a nice house. Just too big for one person," Jerry said, leaving out the fact that having so much space made him miss April and Max even more. "And while the backyard is great, it's a bit lacking in the privacy department."

Fred chuckled. "I told you it's one of ours."

"You did," Jerry agreed.

"So are the houses that flank it. It might look like a quiet neighborhood, but there's enough security surrounding you to get you out in record time."

"Good to know."

"You want a ride?" Fred asked when they reached the street.

"No, it's only a couple of blocks. It'll give me time to wake up a bit before I get behind the wheel."

"Good job out there tonight, McNeal."

"Thanks."

"Oh, and Barney was feeling guilty at giving you a hard time and dropped a little something off at the house to express his apologies."

"Unless that something is a shower and clean bed, it will have to wait until morning."

"I'll tell him you said thanks," Fred said.

Jerry had walked about a block when Houdini barked, and the familiar clopping of hooves filled the air. Jerry looked over his shoulder and saw Tisdale and the dark horse galloping behind him. He turned to greet the man. "Problem?"

"No, Maioriello and Raymond are basking in the sun off the coast of Australia."

"Sounds like a good way to spend the afterlife," Jerry agreed. "I take it Maioriello is keeping his word."

"Looks to be," Tisdale replied.

"What's next for you?"

The ranger patted the horse's neck. "Just going to hang on and see where Laura Bell takes me."

"So, this is the infamous Laura Bell?"

"Yep. She was waiting for me when I crossed over, and we've been together ever since."

"How long ago was that?"

Tisdale sighed. "Too long to remember. Besides, if I told you, you'd know her age, and a lady never likes to talk about things like that."

Jerry laughed. "No, I don't suppose they do. You take care of yourself, Tisdale."

Tisdale tipped his hat. "You too, McNeal. It was good riding the trail with you. Who knows, maybe we'll ride again someday."

"I'd like that," Jerry said sincerely.

"Oh, I nearly forgot. I have something for you." He reached into his saddlebag and took out a harness made of thin braided leather. "Try that out on that pup of yours. You'll find it's adjustable and a bit of a special weave. I guarantee it will hold him in one place if you find the need."

Jerry looked at the braided rope, which looked to be a smaller, thinner version of the one used to tie up Maioriello. He started to thank the man and realized both Tisdale and his horse were gone. It was then he realized he was actually going to miss the man. *You're getting soft in your old age, McNeal.*

***

As Jerry shut the front door of the house, he knew he wasn't alone. He checked the door to the first bedroom, flipped on the light, and found the pink-haired spirit sleeping on top of the covers. Not wishing to deal with her, he pulled the door closed. The dogs bolted, racing each other up the stairs. Jerry ran after them, determined to keep them from claiming his bed. He stormed down the hall, pushed open the door to the master bedroom, and saw both dogs crouched on the edge of the bed, staring at him with K-9 smiles. "Get out of my bed!"

The dogs jumped to the floor as April lifted her head. "Wow, I thought for sure you'd be happy to see me."

The stress of the day caught up with him, and it was all Jerry could do to keep his emotions in check. He sat on the edge of the bed and gathered her in his arms. "What are you doing here?"

"We got worried when Houdini disappeared. I tried to call, but you didn't answer. I called Fred, and he said Houdini was with you. He knew how upset we were, so he sent the Learjet. Barney dropped us off an hour ago."

Us? "Max is here too?"

"Of course. I tried to get her to sleep on the jet, but she was too excited. Fred said we can stay as long as we want, so she's spent the whole trip searching the Internet and writing a list of things she wants us to see. So far, she has the zoo, SeaWorld, the Riverwalk, and the Alamo. She said it was Granny's idea. She told her you never take time to see the things around you."

Jerry realized at that moment that while he'd been at the front door of the Alamo, he'd never even taken a second to peek inside. "That sounds like a grand idea. There is a Texas Ranger museum nearby. I'd like to add that to the list."

"It's already there, along with several restaurants. She found one that is themed and all the waitstaff dress up, and one that serves a pizza that will barely fit on the table."

"You had me at pizza," Jerry said, kissing the top of her head. "I'm glad you're here. This house felt lonely when I thought I'd be staying here alone."

April giggled.

Jerry pulled back. "What's so funny?"

"You weren't going to be here alone. Max said to tell you that Bunny is sleeping in the guest room."

"Bunny? The pink-haired lady?"

"That's the one. You called her the Easter Bunny. Turns out her name really is Bunny."

"Does Max know why she's here?"

"Nope, but she promised the woman she would help her figure it out."

Jerry swelled with pride. "That means Max has her very first case."

April beamed. "Yep, she's just like her dad."

Jerry felt the bubble burst.

April rubbed the crease on his forehead. "I was talking about you. She told me not to tell you, but she considers you her dad."

"Why doesn't she want me to know?"

"Why do you think? Fear of rejection."

"I would never push her away."

"Don't get upset. She's thirteen."

"I'm not upset. I'm stoked. If I wasn't a man's man, I'd cry."

April giggled.

"What? You don't think I'm a man's man?"

"Of course I do. I also think you are kind and considerate, which is why we love you. There's only one problem," she said, pushing him away. "You stink."

Jerry sniffed his underarms. "I do, don't I?"

"Yes. If you want to sleep in my bed, you'll have to shower first."

Jerry lifted a brow. "I claimed it first."

April lifted the covers. "Fine, there are plenty of others to choose from."

"Don't you dare move. I'll be out in a jiff."

***

The water felt so good that Jerry ended up staying in the shower longer than he intended. By the time he was done, April was sound asleep. He walked down the hall and peeked in the room to check on Max. Both Gunter and Houdini shared her bed. Gunter's tail thumped as Jerry stood in the doorway. *Good boy, Gunter. Take care of our girl.*

"Night, Dad." Max's whisper was barely audible.

"Night, Little Girl," Jerry said, pulling the door closed. He returned to his room and stood listening to April's soft, easy breaths. As he climbed into bed beside her, he realized that never in all his years had he felt so complete.

***

Jerry woke to the sound of water running in the shower. He lingered under the covers, waiting for

April to finish. As he lay there thinking of the possibilities, he felt a hand on his shoulder. Confused, he turned.

Bunny greeted him with a wrinkled fuchsia grin.

While Jerry was reluctant to have a woman see him cry, he had no such qualms having one hear him scream.

Bunny popped him on the forehead. "Quit being so dramatic, hot stuff. I'm not here to take advantage of you. I just wanted to tell you what a smart kid you've got there. She was here five minutes and already helped me remember my name. She said she'll help me figure out why I'm here so I can move on, but if it's all the same with you, I think I'll hang around for a while."

The End

Next up is *Merry Me*, book 15 in The Jerry McNeal Series, which is set in the Christmas town of Frankenmuth Michigan.

https://www.amazon.com/dp/B0CHH8NRX2

The eBook is on preorder for May 15th 2024. This is only a placement date as I expect to release the book (in both print and e-book) much earlier.

Please take a moment to head over to my website to sign up for my newsletter, which will keep you informed on the new date and keep you up to date with my writings and expected new releases.

https://www.sherryaburton.com/

About the Author

Sherry A. Burton writes in multiple genres and has won numerous awards for her books. Sherry's awards include the coveted Charles Loring Brace Award, for historical accuracy within her historical fiction series, The Orphan Train Saga. Sherry is a member of the National Orphan Train Society, presents lectures on the history of the orphan trains, and is listed on the NOTC Speaker's Bureau as an approved speaker.

Originally from Kentucky, Sherry and her Retired Navy Husband now call Michigan home. Sherry enjoys traveling and spending time with her husband of more than forty years.